"That day all those *horrible things you* *you mean them?"*

"No," Beau said softly. "I didn't mean them."

Starr let out a long sigh. "I knew it. But…why?"

All these years he'd nursed a hopeless yearning that someday they'd talk about this. And here they were, and it was happening just the way he'd always dreamed it….

He said, "I only knew then that I was headed for a bad place and I had to make sure you didn't try to follow me there."

"Oh," she said softly. "Well, it worked. Because it made me see that I had to make some changes or I could end up…" She didn't seem to know how to finish.

So Beau did it for her. "…Following the wrong guy down the road to nowhere?"

Tears welled in Starr's eyes as she turned to him again. "Yes, I guess that's it. But look…I didn't go down that road. And you…well, Beau. You have done it. You've found your way back."

Dear Reader,

Well, June may be the traditional month for weddings, but we here at Silhouette find June is busting out all over—with babies! We begin with Christine Rimmer's *Fifty Ways To Say I'm Pregnant.* When bound-for-the-big-city Starr Bravo shares a night of passion with the rancher she's always loved, she finds herself in the family way. But how to tell him? *Fifty Ways* is a continuation of Christine's Bravo Family saga, so look for the BRAVO FAMILY TIES flash. And for those of you who remember Christine's JONES GANG series, you'll be delighted with the cameo appearance of an old friend....

Next, Joan Elliott Pickart continues her miniseries THE BABY BET: MACALLISTER'S GIFTS with *Accidental Family,* the story of a day-care center worker and a single dad with amnesia who find themselves falling for each other as she cares for their children together. And there's another CAVANAUGH JUSTICE offering in Special Edition from Marie Ferrarella: in *Cavanaugh's Woman,* an actress researching a film role needs a top cop— and Shaw Cavanaugh fits the bill nicely. *Hot August Nights* by Christine Flynn continues THE KENDRICKS OF CAMELOT miniseries, in which the reserved, poised Kendrick daughter finds her one-night stand with the town playboy coming back to haunt her in a big way. Janis Reams Hudson begins MEN OF CHEROKEE ROSE with *The Daddy Survey,* in which two little girls go all out to get their mother a new husband. And don't miss *One Perfect Man,* in which almost-new author Lynda Sandoval tells the story of a career-minded events planner who has never had time for romance until she gets roped into planning a party for the daughter of a devastatingly handsome single father. So enjoy the rising temperatures, all six of these wonderful romances...and don't forget to come back next month for six more, in Silhouette Special Edition.

Happy Reading!

Gail Chasan
Senior Editor

Please address questions and book requests to:
Silhouette Reader Service
U.S.: 3010 Walden Ave., P.O. Box 1325, Buffalo, NY 14269
Canadian: P.O. Box 609, Fort Erie, Ont. L2A 5X3

Christine Rimmer

FIFTY WAYS TO SAY I'M PREGNANT

Silhouette

SPECIAL EDITION

Published by Silhouette Books

America's Publisher of Contemporary Romance

For all those wonderful readers who wouldn't quit asking, "But what about Beau and Starr…?"

 SILHOUETTE BOOKS

ISBN 0-373-24615-3

FIFTY WAYS TO SAY I'M PREGNANT

Copyright © 2004 by Christine Rimmer

Books by Christine Rimmer

CHRISTINE RIMMER

came to her profession the long way around. Before settling down to write about the magic of romance, she'd been everything from an actress to a phone sales representative to a playwright. Christine is grateful not only for the joy she finds in writing, but for what waits when the day's work is through: a man she loves, who loves her right back, and the privilege of watching their children grow and change day to day. She lives with her family in Oklahoma.

Prologue

Starr Bravo, home for the summer after her first year of college, stood at the kitchen sink peeling carrots for the stew already simmering on the stove.

"Stah light, stah bwight," chanted a small voice not far from her feet. Starr had tried teaching her half brother, Ethan, the children's rhyme just last night. The toddler remembered the first part and seemed to think it referred to his big sister, personally. "Stah light, stah bwight..." Something with wheels rolled up the back of her bare leg.

"Hey!" She paused with a carrot half-peeled to glance over her shoulder and fake a scowl at him.

He beamed up at her as he rolled his tiny toy truck back down the side of her calf. "Vrrooom, vroom..."

"Stop that." The words were firm, but she couldn't keep an adoring grin from pulling at the corners of her mouth.

"Vroom, vroom…" Ethan rolled the little truck off across the floor, fat legs working at a speedy crawl.

Starr's stepmother, Tess, was sitting at the long pine table snapping beans, Edna Heller at her side. Years ago, Edna had been the Rising Sun Ranch's house-keeper, but now the slim woman in her late fifties was just plain family—and Ethan, *vrooming* with enthusi-asm, had his toy truck rolling straight for her left foot.

Edna crossed her ankles and scooted them under her chair. "Don't you even try it, young man."

"Vroom, vroom, vroom…"

Starr turned back to her carrot, peeled it swiftly clean and set it on the counter, smiling to herself, thinking how good it was to be home.

Out the window, past the flattened patches of still-green grass and the slanting roofs of the barn and the sheds, she could see the snowy crests of the Bighorn Mountains in the distance, swathed in a few white wisps of cloud. The green slopes of rolling prairie land, dotted here and there with stands of cotton-woods, lay spread below the mountains in overlapping swells of sun and shadow. Closer still, in the pasture behind the barn, a windmill whirled in the afternoon breeze, the sun catching in its vanes, making a golden blur.

As she reached for the next carrot in the pile, a pickup truck—dark green and caked with mud—rolled into the rear yard. Starr spotted the driver and forgot all about that next carrot.

Beau Tisdale.

She dropped her peeler in the sink.

Bold as you please, he pushed open the driver's door and jumped to the ground. He wore dusty Wranglers and dustier boots, a faded chambray work shirt, sweat-dark along his chest, under the arms and down his back. His battered straw Resistol shaded his features, but she knew him, anyway. Knew the strong, wide set of his shoulders, the lean hard waist, the long, muscled legs....

Yeah, she knew him. Though she damn well wished she didn't.

At the table, Ethan was driving his miniature truck in and out between the chairs. "Vroom, vroom, vroom," he growled as he went.

Tess laughed. "Ethan John, you will get yourself stepped on."

"Vroom, vrrrooom, vrroooommmm…"

Outside, some other cowpuncher Starr didn't recognize got out on the passenger side and went around to the tailgate. Beau joined him. The two of them pulled on work gloves and started unloading the fencing wire and posts piled high in the pickup's bed. Quickly and methodically, they set to stacking everything against the side of the barn.

Starr watched them for a while, kind of simmering inside. In spite of being a rotten lying jerk as a person, Beau was a good worker, strong and always with his mind on the job, never a wasted movement. She could practically see the muscles flexing under that sweat-stained shirt....

She grabbed a towel. "Beau Tisdale is here." Wiping her hands, she turned to the women at the table, trying with all her might to keep her voice offhand. "He's got a pickup piled with fence wire and posts, which he is in the process of unloading as I speak."

Tess and Edna shared a look—and then they both

went back to snapping those beans. "Oh, yes," said Tess, her eyes on the bean she was snapping and her voice as studiously casual as Starr's had tried to be. "Daniel got some kind of deal from the suppliers on fixed-knot fence. It's more expensive than barb wire, but safer for the stock. Lasts longer, too, they say. Daniel and Beau convinced your father to give it a try. So I'd imagine Beau's just bringing some of it by."

Daniel Hart, an old guy with no family to speak of, owned a nearby ranch. A couple of years ago, when Beau was fresh out of the slammer, he'd hired on with Mr. Hart. The job, evidently, had worked out just fine.

"Well, isn't that just so *helpful* of Beau," Starr said, ladling on the saccharine. She tipped her chin at a defiant angle. Yeah, she had an attitude when it came to Beau—and she didn't care who knew it, either.

"Yes, it is," said her stepmother, curly head bowed over those beans. "Very helpful."

Tossing the towel aside, Starr whirled back to the window and snatched up her peeler. *Slammer,* she thought the word again, with relish, as she grabbed the next carrot and began scraping away. Fresh out of the *slammer*…

She made short work of the carrot and the next one, too. In no time the carrots were all done. She started in on a big potato. Beyond the window, Beau and the unknown cowboy were unloading the last of the fencing materials.

And okay, if you wanted to be strictly factual about it, Beau had gone to the state honor farm and not the penitentiary when he did his time. He'd gotten that break because both Tess and Zach, Starr's dad, had spoken up for him at the trial. Starr only called it the slammer secretly, to herself. Yeah, it was mean-spirited of her—but she figured she had a right to be a little bit mean-spirited where Beau Tisdale was concerned.

Her father had done a lot for Beau, standing up for him in court like that, after what Beau did. And then, when Beau got out, her dad had been the one who set him up with the job at the Hart place.

Ferociously, Starr scraped away potato skin, baring the naked white meat beneath.

And this wasn't the first time in the past few years that she'd seen Beau around the Rising Sun. She gouged at one of the stubborn eyes that dotted the otherwise smooth-peeled surface. Oh, yeah, she'd seen him and her dad together, out leaning on the horse pasture fence, side by side. And more than once, she'd spotted Beau riding in with the hands after a long day's work poisoning weeds or scattering bulls or doing God knew what all.

Yeah, okay. In a lot of ways, ranching was a community endeavor. Folks from different ranches worked together to get the tough stuff done. But this was more than that. When she was home for Easter, she'd even seen her dad patting Beau on the back. A *friendly* gesture. Like they were good pals or something....

Tess and her dad were fine people. They would always do what they could to help the disadvantaged. Starr was proud of them for that, and she had no problem with them making it so Beau didn't have to do hard time. She could even accept her dad's finding him a job, giving him a new start.

But her dad making *friends* with him? That was one step too far.

"You're going to mangle that poor potato until there's not a thing left of it."

Starr froze in midgouge. She'd been so absorbed in her fury at Beau, she hadn't even heard her stepmother approach.

"Starr…" Tess's soft voice soothed and reproached at the same time. Starr gritted her teeth and went on gouging eyes—until Tess's slim, work-roughened hand came around and settled over her own. "Come on, give me that potato.…"

Outside, Beau and the other hand were getting back into the cab. Doors slammed, one and then the other.

"Starr…"

"Fine. Take it." She slapped the potato into Tess's hand and threw the peeler in the sink. Outside, the dirty green pickup drove off. Flipping on the tap, she swiftly rinsed her hands and grabbed for the towel again. "I could use a break, anyway."

She tossed the towel on the counter and marched out of there, ignoring the way Ethan sat chewing on his toy truck, staring at her with wide, bewildered eyes and Edna pursed up her mouth and shook her head over her beans—and Tess just stood there, looking worried, the peeled, gouged potato still cradled in her hand.

About five minutes later, Starr heard a careful tap on her door. "Starr?" Tess's voice.

By then, Starr was beginning to feel just a little bit ashamed. No matter how angry it got her to see Beau Tisdale making himself at home on the Rising Sun, she shouldn't have gone off like that. She wasn't the sulky, messed-up kid she'd once been. Now, besides being someone you could count on and a straight-A student, she took pride in being the kind of person who never descended to throwing fits, or flying off the handle when something bugged her.

"May I come in?" Tess asked from the other side of the door.

"Yeah," Starr said grudgingly. "Okay, come on."

Tess slipped around the door and closed it behind her by leaning back against it, one hand still on the knob. "You okay?"

Starr let a good thirty seconds elapse before answering. She spent the time tugging at the hem of her shorts and pretending to study the swirling blue-and-purple pattern on her bedspread. Tess had sewn the spread for her—along with the dark blue curtains—when Starr was sixteen and came back to live at the Rising Sun.

"Yeah," Starr gave out, at last. "I'm okay."

Cautiously, Tess approached the bed. Starr signaled her willingness to talk by sliding over and making a space for her. Tess took the space, settling into it so gently that the mattress hardly shifted.

After that, for a minute or two, they just sat there, neither seeming to know quite where to begin.

Tess broke the silence. "Those curtains..." She nudged Starr and indicated the curtains she had made three years before. "I was hanging them when I looked down into the rear yard and saw you and Beau going into the barn...."

"God." Starr dropped her head back and groaned at the ceiling. "Do you have to remind me of that day—let alone of that guy?"

Tess wrapped an arm around her shoulder and gave

an encouraging squeeze. "Well, yes. I think I do. I think maybe this is something we've waited a little too long to talk about."

Hurt welled up, making her throat feel too tight. She jerked out of the comforting circle of Tess's arm and hitched a leg up on the bed, facing her stepmother more fully. "I just don't get it, you know? Dad's like…his *friend* now. How can Dad do that, after what Beau Tisdale did to me?"

"Oh, honey…" Tess reached out again.

Starr ducked away. "Uh-uh. Don't try to make it all better. It's not all better. You were there. You were the one who caught us together. And you were there later, too, in the yard, after Dad told him to go. You saw how he threw my heart down on the ground and stomped on it with his worn-out old boot."

"Starr—"

Starr threw up both hands. "Don't…make any excuses for him."

"But I—"

"Uh-uh. No." They stared at each other, and then Starr allowed, "Okay. I know it wasn't really his fault, that thing with his awful brothers making him sit point for them while they rustled our cattle. I know he turned it around there at the end, went against his brothers and helped you take them in. I can understand, I really can, why you and Dad stood up for him at court over that. And why Dad set him up with old man Hart. But the other…what happened the day before you and Dad caught Beau and his brothers out by the Farley breaks. What happened…with Beau and me…" The old hurt felt so new and fresh at that moment, it closed off her throat and stole the rest of the words right out of her mouth. She hung her head and blinked back tears—stupid, pointless tears, for a man who didn't deserve them.

Light as warm breeze, Tess's hand stroked her hair. Starr lifted her head. "Tess, I *trusted* him—and three years ago, you know how I was. I didn't trust anyone then. But I did trust Beau. And he took my trust and threw it back in my face."

Tess spoke softly. "Honey, I think there was more to it than that. I think it's time you started to look at what happened through the eyes of a woman, because you are becoming a woman now, and a fine one. You are no longer that same hurt, confused girl you were then."

"What are you talking about? You were there. You saw. He did it right out in the yard, with you and Dad and probably Edna and any ranch hand who bothered to look out his trailer window watching while it happened."

"Starr—"

"No!" She shook her head, hard. "How can you make excuses for him? You know what he did." Oh, she could still remember it like it was yesterday—a hot day, in June, a day kind of like this one....

Her own heart pounding hard in her ears, Starr came running down the stairs, Tess following after her. She ran straight through the great room and out to the entrance hall, flinging back the front door and racing out to the porch.

Across the yard, the door to Beau's trailer opened. Her dad came out. He started up the driveway, heading for the back of the house. But when he saw her on the porch, he changed direction and came straight to the foot of the front steps. "What's the matter?"

Starr leaned on the porch rail, tears pushing at the back of her throat. "Daddy, what happened? Did you talk to him? Did he tell you—?"

"Starr." Her dad had a tired look, his tanned face drawn and tight-lipped. "I thought you said you'd stay in your room."

"I couldn't," she cried. "I had to know. Did he tell you, how we have something special between us? Do you understand now that he never meant anything wrong to happen, that he—?"

"Starr. Beau is leaving. I'm going to go get his pay and then he'll be gone."

She couldn't believe what she was hearing. She gaped at her father. "What? No. You can't do that. That's not right, not fair…" She pushed away from the railing and darted to the steps.

Her dad blocked her path. "Go back upstairs."

Why wouldn't he understand? Why couldn't he see? "I have to talk to him."

"No, you don't. Just let the damn fool go."

Hot fury swirled through her, that he would speak of Beau that way. "He is not a fool! He…he cares for me, that's all. He just wanted to be with me, like I want to be with him."

It was all there in her dad's sad eyes: that she was sixteen and Beau was twenty-one, that she was a Bravo and Beau was one of those shiftless, no-good Tisdales.…

Unfair. It was so unfair. She'd *told* him that she'd never had sex with any guy, whatever everybody seemed to think of her—that she and Beau hadn't done anything but kissing out there in the barn, that, yeah, Beau had unbuttoned her shirt. But that was all. It hadn't gone any further.

"Starr," her dad said. "Go upstairs."

No way. She dodged to slide around him, but he seemed to sense she would do it and stepped in her path once more. She ran square into his chest as he grabbed her by both arms.

"No!" she cried, shouting now. She had to get through him, had to get to Beau. "Let me go!" she screamed. "Let me talk to him!"

"Starr, listen." Her dad's big hands held on tight, though she kicked and squirmed and beat on his chest. "Starr. Settle down."

She was wild by then, twisting and flailing. "No! I won't! I won't! Let me go!"

From behind her, Tess said, "He's coming."

Her dad swore. Starr froze and craned around him to see. Beau was coming out of his trailer across the yard. "Beau!" she called, all her desperate yearning there in his name. "Beau, he won't let me talk to you!" She tried again to break free, catching her dad off-guard, sliding around him, almost succeeding that time. But somehow, he managed to catch one arm as she flew by. He hauled her back against his chest, grabbing the other arm, too, holding her like that, with her arms behind her as she yanked and squirmed and tried to kick back at him, to get herself free, to run to Beau.

Beau came at them, fast, long strides stirring the dirt under his boots. He stopped a few feet from where Starr stood, with her father holding her arms and her body yearning toward him.

She saw the bruise then—a big, mean one on Beau's chin, and she gasped in outrage. "Beau. He *hit* you!" She turned a hot glare over her shoulder, at her dad.

Beau said, his voice flat with no caring in it, "Forget it. It's nothing."

She swung her head front, facing Beau again and she gave him her outrage, her fury for his sake. "No. He had no right to hit you! You didn't do anything wrong. He can't—"

"Starr." His eyes were so cold. She couldn't see the man she'd thought she loved in them anywhere. "He had a right."

"No!" It came out all ragged, a cry of pure distress. She'd stopped struggling to get free of her dad's grip. Now, she just stood there and looked at Beau, at his dead eyes and his expressionless face. *Oh, where are you?* her heart cried. *Where have you gone to? What are you telling me?*

Slowly, Beau smiled. A knowing smile—knowing and ugly. And then, very low, he chuckled. It was a dirty, insulting sound.

"Tisdale," her dad warned in a growl.

"Zach," Tess said from back on the porch. "Let him tell her."

For a moment nothing happened, then, with no warning, her dad let go of her. She staggered a little at the sudden lack of restraint and reached out toward Beau. "Beau, please—"

He cut her off, his tone evil with nasty, intimate humor. "You thought you'd heard every line, didn't you, big-city girl? Heard 'em all and never fell for a one. But the lonesome cowboy routine got you goin', didn't it?"

This couldn't be happening. "Wh—what are you saying?"

He made a low, smug sound. "You know damn well what I'm saying."

She shook her head, fiercely, as if she could shake his cruel words right out of her head. "No...."

"'Fraid so." Beau lowered his voice, as if sharing a dirty secret with her. "Come on, you know how guys are."

Starr kept shaking her head. "No! You wouldn't. You *couldn't*. All those things you said—"

He shrugged. "They didn't mean squat. I was after one thing. And we both know what that was."

"No..." She only got it out on a whisper that time.

Beau went on smiling that mean, hurtful smile. "Yeah."

Her dad cut in then. "Okay, enough. Go on, Tisdale. Around back. I'll get your money."

And without another word to her, Beau turned and walked away.

"It hurt, Tess," Starr said, softly now, head bowed again, shoulders slumped. "I don't think you know how much it hurt...."

Tess didn't argue. She only reached out and brushed a hand against Starr's arm, a gesture that spoke better than words could have—of comfort, of understanding....

Starr faced her stepmother again. "And it...shamed me, so bad. To have him say those terrible things. And right in front of everyone, too."

"I know it did," Tess whispered. "And...I am so sorry."

Starr made a low sound. "Don't be. It wasn't your fault."

Tess pressed her lips together. And then she sighed. "You're wrong there. It *was* my fault. At least a little."

"But how?" Starr blinked. "No. I don't see how you can say that."

Tess sat up just a fraction straighter. "I say it because it's true. Zach would have stopped Beau from saying those things. But I told your father to let Beau go ahead." She paused, looking deeply into Starr's eyes. "Don't you remember?"

Starr looked away. She was back out in the yard again, on that day three years ago, in the process of getting her poor heart broken. *"Zach,"* Tess had said. *"Let him tell her...."*

"Yeah." She turned to Tess again. "I remember. But that doesn't put you at fault."

Tess raised a hand. "Yes. In a way, it does. Because I knew what Beau would say. I knew what he was trying to do. And I thought it was the best thing for you, to go ahead and let him do it. Let him hurt and shame you so bad that your powerful feeling for him would sour into hate, that you'd never want to speak to him again, and most important, that you wouldn't go ruining your life chasing after him...."

"Well, so? You were right. I needed to hear him say what he said. I needed to hear from his own lying mouth what a dirty low-down rat he is. You had it right, that's all. If he hadn't said those things, I just might have wrecked my life running after him."

"But you didn't run after him," Tess said with a rueful kind of smile half curving her mouth. "And since then, you've pretty much turned your life around, haven't you?''

"Well, yeah." She made a humphing sound. She *had* been flunking school the year before, running pretty wild down in San Diego, with the money her mother threw at her to keep her out of her hair—and no supervision at all. "Okay," she admitted. "I guess in a twisted sort of way, Beau did me a favor. Those rotten things he said made me want nothing to do with him. And since he landed himself in jail not long after that, it was the best thing that could have happened to me. I set my mind on making my life something better than it was then. So, okay. If you look it that way, he did me a big favor.''

Tess's smile stretched a little wider. "He did, didn't he?''

"But it doesn't make him any less of a creep. Yeah, he helped me, in a backhanded way. But it wasn't like he said those things for my sake or anything.''

Tess wasn't smiling by then. "But Starr. What if that's exactly what he did? What if he hurt you because he knew it would set you free?''

Starr blinked and scooted back a little. She had a shivery feeling down inside, a kind of giddy strangeness in her stomach. "No. You don't really think…''

"Yes, I do. I suspected it then. But now, after seeing the way he's managed to make something of his own life against near-impossible odds, I'm pretty much positive he said what he said for your sake. He knew he was in big trouble, Starr. His brothers were up to no good, and they'd been battering and abusing him for so long, he had a real hard time standing up to them. He was headed for trouble with the law, and he knew it—and he didn't want to drag you down with him.''

The hurt, cold place at the center of her heart felt somehow a little bit warmer right then. ''You think?''

''I do.'' Tess reached out and pressed a loving hand against the side of Starr's face. ''So. Maybe you can find it in your heart to forgive the guy a little?''

Starr took Tess's cradling hand and gave it a squeeze before letting go. ''You know, you are...a real mom to me.''

Tess's lower lip trembled just a little. ''Why, honey. What a beautiful thing to say.''

''It's only the truth—and I know how you are. So respectful of my mother's place in my life. So I want you to know it's nothing against my mother's memory, I promise.'' Starr's natural mother had lived in San Diego with her much-older, very wealthy second husband—until she'd died in a freeway pileup two years before. When Starr thought of Leila Wickerston Bravo Marks, it was always with a feeling of sad regret—that they'd never shared the kind of closeness that Starr had with Tess, that her mother had never understood her and never had much time for her. Leila had lavished money on Starr, but love and attention were always in short supply.

''My mother was my mother,'' Starr said, trying not to sound as grim as the subject always made her feel. ''I know that—and about Beau...''

''Umm?''

''I'll think about what you said. I can kind of see the sense in it. And I do know that Beau has worked hard to make a life for himself after the mess he started out with. I guess he doesn't need to have me staring daggers at his back every time he comes around.''

Tess leaned close enough to brush a kiss right between Starr's eyes. When she pulled back, a tear was trailing down her soft cheek. She swiped it away with the back of a hand. ''I am so proud of you. And so is your dad.'' She reached out again and smoothed a hank of Starr's hair, guiding it back behind her ear. Then she grinned. ''But I have to say, I kind of miss that rhinestone you used wear in your nose.''

Starr gave her a sideways look. ''Hey. I've still got the navel ring—and a tiny ladybug tattoo right on my—''

''Don't—'' Tess put up a hand ''—mention that to your dad.''

Starr wiggled her eyebrows. ''He doesn't ask, I don't tell…''

Tess laughed at that, a happy, trilling laugh. Starr thought how good it was to know her, that Tess was not only the mother she'd always needed, Tess was also a true friend. Tess jumped off the bed. ''Come on.'' She brushed at the front of her jeans, as if they'd managed to get wrinkles in them somehow. ''There are beans to snap, potatoes to peel—and tonight, if you're lucky, you, Jobeth, Edna and I will fight to the death in a brutal game of Scrabble.'' Jobeth was Tess's daughter by her first husband. She was eleven now, and right where she wanted to be—out with Zach, who had adopted her that first year he and Tess got together. Jobeth loved every aspect of ranching, from pulling calves to branding to gathering day.

Starr groaned. "It's a thrill a minute around this place."

Tess was already at the door. "Coming?"

Starr smiled then. "You know what? It's great to be home."

Chapter One

Three years later...

Blame it on that sliver of moon hanging from a star in the summer sky. Blame it on the two beers he had that he probably shouldn't have. Blame it on the sight of her—that black hair shining like a crow's wing by the light of the paper lanterns strung overhead, those eyes that unforgettable heart-stopping amethyst-blue. Blame it on the yearning inside him, the yearning that, after all those years, still remained with him, tender as an old wound that never did heal quite right.

Blame it on...

Hell. Blame it on whatever you damn well please.

At the annual Medicine Creek Merchant Society's Independence Day dance, out under the stars in Patriot Park, after six endless years of keeping strictly away from her, Beau Tisdale decided he would ask Starr Bravo for a dance.

It was no picnic mustering the courage to do it. He stood for a while under the night-shadowed branches of a cottonwood a ways from the bunting-draped temporary dance floor, nursing a third longneck, watching her as he worked up his nerve.

Twice, she danced with Barnaby Cotes, the sneaky weasel who ran Cotes Clothing and Gift on Main Street and was too old for her by half. Then Tim Cally, a hand on the Rising Sun for decades, led her out on the floor. Beau smiled at that. Tim was nearing sixty and a little stiff in the joints, but he could still do a fair two-step. He held Starr lightly and not too close. Beau didn't mind watching that—not that he had any right to mind or not to mind where Starr was concerned.

He tipped up the longneck and took a deep drink. Just one damn dance, he was thinking. What can it hurt?

Stupid question. It'd hurt plenty if those violet eyes went to ice on him, if she turned him down flat. A man does have his pride, after all.

But he didn't guess she'd begrudge him a dance. She'd seemed civil enough to him in the last few years. When he'd pass her on the street or see her on the Rising Sun, she'd give him a cool smile and a nod, anyway. If he was lucky, he'd even get a plain, politely spoken, "Hi, Beau."

She never seemed overjoyed to set eyes on him, but it wasn't near as bad as it had been those first couple of years after he got off the honor farm. In those years, when she looked at him, he felt knee-high to a skunk and twice as foul-smelling. She'd hated him then, pure and simple, for the hard and heartless things he'd said to her that day in the yard at the Rising Sun.

But she didn't seem to hate him anymore. Maybe she'd figured out a few things. Or maybe it was just a long time down a dusty road and what some cowboy had said to her six years ago when she was still a girl didn't mean a thing to her now.

No, he couldn't say she was exactly falling all over herself to get next to him in recent years. But if he asked for a dance, he figured he had at least a fifty-fifty chance she'd say yes….

She sat out the next dance, another two-step, strolling instead over to one of the picnic tables not far from the bandstand to take her place with Tess and Zach and Jobeth. Zach's cousin Nate Bravo sat with them, along with his wife Meggie May, who was round as a corn-fed hen with their third child. Zach had told him the other day that Tess was pregnant, too. "Three months along," Zach had said quietly, pride and happiness glowing in his eyes.

As Beau watched, Jobeth ducked low, hunching her shoulders to the table, as if she'd like to melt right on through the rough wood planks. And Starr, sitting next to her, threw back her shining head and laughed.

Beau stood transfixed at the free, joyous sound. The band played on, a fast one, but Starr Bravo's laugh was a whole other kind of music, the very sweetest kind. Jobeth elbowed her stepsister in the side and Starr made a show of composing herself. Jobeth straightened. In the light of the red, white and blue lanterns overhead, Jobeth's face looked more than a little bit flushed. She said something snappish to Starr, who leaned sideways enough to bump her shoulder in the affectionate way that a sister will do. Jobeth still looked mulish, but Beau could see the reluctant smile that twitched the corners of her mouth.

About then, Beau caught sight of Nick Collerby lurking near the Bravo table. The dark-haired kid was about Jobeth's age and had teased and tormented Starr's sister from elementary school onward. Maybe Jobeth was worried he might ask her to dance.

And the toe-tapping song was ending. If he didn't hustle his butt over there, some other lucky cowhand would be getting the next dance with Starr. Beau drained the last of his beer and chucked the empty in a recycling can as he went by. He walked fast, hoping speed would get him where he was going before he lost his nerve. As a result, in no time at all, he found himself standing right there by the table full of Bravos.

Tess and Meggie beamed up at him.

"Hi, Beau."

"How're you doin'?"

His throat felt like it had a fence post lodged in it. He cleared it, raising his hat in a polite salute and then settling it back in place. "Well, I'm fine. Just fine."

"Nice night," said Zach.

"Yeah. Real nice."

About then, Jobeth giggled into her hand. A sideways glance and he saw that Starr was the one giving *her* the elbow, that time.

"Where's Daniel?" asked Tess. "He always enjoys a celebration. I'd have thought he'd come out tonight."

To keep his gaze from lingering too long on Starr, Beau made himself focus on Zach's pretty wife.

"Daniel's feeling a little under the weather." Beau had left the older man in his ancient easy chair, reading *Western Horseman,* looking kind of pale, vowing there was nothing wrong with him that a few antacids and a good night's rest wouldn't cure.

Twin lines of concern formed between Tess's smooth brows. "Nothing serious, I hope?"

"He says he's just tired. But I'm keeping my eye on him."

Tess smiled her gentle smile. "Good. He needs someone to look out for him a little. He pushes himself too hard sometimes."

"That he does." The band struck up the next number. A slow one. It was now or never. "Ahem. Starr, I wonder if I might have this dance?"

The second the words were out, he wanted to suck them right back in. They couldn't have sounded stiffer if he was a damn corpse. He'd meant to be casual and easy. *How 'bout a dance?* maybe, or *Come on. Let's dance....*

Jobeth giggled again. If he'd had a pistol on him, he'd have fired a shot past her head just to shut that girl up. And then the giggle ended on a sharp, startled, "Oh!" She scowled at her sister and he put it together. Starr must have kicked her under the table.

And Starr was...getting up. It was going to happen. He would have his dance. "Sure, Beau. That would be nice." God bless America, was there ever a woman so blasted beautiful? She'd let that inky hair, once chopped and spiky, grow long. It flowed past her shoulders when she wore it loose, but tonight it was anchored up at the back, little wisps of it kissing her velvety cheeks. And those eyes...

They were the eyes he saw in his dreams, lupine-blue. His breath was all tangled up in his chest. His heart stopped—and then set to pounding like a herd of spooked mustangs.

She walked around the table toward him, not smiling exactly, but friendly enough. Her snug red top hooked at one shoulder, leaving the other bare, revealing skin so pure and fine-textured, it seemed to glow in the lantern light.

She held out her hand and the mustangs in his chest started bucking and snorting. Damn, he was a sad case for certain.

Her hand was slim and smooth and cool. His own felt hot and he knew it was rough. But she didn't seem to mind.

Her smile bloomed wide. The wild horses inside him went suddenly calm as he smiled back. "Come on, then," she said. He let her lead the way across the flattened grass of the clearing and up the two steps to the dance floor.

She tucked herself into his arms as if she'd been born to be there. Between that red top and her low-riding jeans, a narrow section of bare waist tempted him. She was never going to know how powerfully he wanted to ease his fingers under the stretchy material and wrap his hand around that silky inward curve....

Uh-uh. He grasped her waist lightly, and his fingers didn't stray where they had no right to go. He breathed in the scent of her. It was as he remembered it, hinting of some wonderful exotic flower, causing an old memory to stir...

Jasmine, he thought. She smells like jasmine.

Years and years before, when he was six or maybe

seven, his mother had dared to try and leave his father. She'd taken Beau with her, to her people in Arkansas. On the cyclone fence in his grandmother's side yard, grew a lush green vine thick with tiny trumpet-shaped flowers, the sweet scent so heady he would ignore the bees that swarmed over it, just to get close and breathe in their perfume. "That's jasmine, Beau, sweetie," his mother had told him, bending close, that heart-shaped gold locket she always wore falling out on its chain, gleaming in the sunlight.

His father had come after them soon enough and brought them back. And Beau had never smelled jasmine again.

Until Starr.

Careful, he thought. Don't hold her too close….

For a moment or two, they simply danced, her head tucked against his shoulder, her scent enticing him, the feel of her under his hands making all his senses spin.

Then she lifted her head and met his eyes. "So…how've you been?" It was a safe, general-type question and he found he was grateful to her for asking it. Talking was good. It kept him from getting too lost in the feel and the smell of her.

"Working," he said. "Keeping my nose clean."

She tipped her head to the side. The wisps of midnight hair stirred against her cheeks. "Happy?"

The question, for some reason, seemed unbearably personal—intimate, even. As if she asked for the secrets in his deepest heart. His gut tightened and he almost missed a step. But he recovered. He pulled her a bit closer and felt the tips of her full breasts brush his chest. His Wranglers got tighter. *Down, damn it,* he thought. "I'm doin' okay." It sounded easy and offhand. Relief curled through him that his voice had not betrayed him. He relaxed again. "You?"

She shrugged, one slim shoulder—the gleaming bare one—lifting, her slim waist shifting a fraction beneath his careful hand. "Yeah. I am." She grinned, as if the thought pleased her. "I'm happy."

"Heard you graduated from C.U. last month."

"That's right. B.A. in journalism. Dean's honor list." She chuckled. "And yes, I am bragging."

"You got the right. It's a big accomplishment." A few years before, with Daniel's encouragement, he'd managed to pass his high school equivalency. But he didn't say that. Yeah, it was a major step for him. He hadn't made it past the ninth grade and he'd never expected to get a chance to go back. But a high school diploma looked pretty puny alongside a college degree. "I think Zach mentioned you were heading to New York City in the fall...."

"That's right. Grandmother Elaine pulled some strings." Zach's parents lived in New York. "*CityWide Magazine*," she said. "It's a weekly. I'll start as an editorial assistant right after Labor Day."

"Well," he said, striving for words that were brilliant and meaningful and finding nothing but, "that sounds just great."

"And for the summer, as usual, I'll be at Jerry Esponda's beck and call." For as long as Beau could remember, Jerry had been publisher, editor-in-chief, reporter and printer of the local weekly *The Medicine Creek Clarion.* No doubt he appreciated Starr's help every summer.

"Jerry'll be real sorry to see you go."

"Well," she said pertly. "I'm not gone yet."

"Soon enough, though."

"Yeah," she softly agreed. "Soon enough." She tucked her head back into his shoulder and they danced the rest of the song without speaking.

As they swayed to the music, he thought about how much things had changed since the last time he'd held her in his arms. She greeted the world with an open, easy smile now. She had her college degree and he had no doubt she would make it in the big city. And he...

Well, he was as free as a man can ever get from the wrongs he'd done in the past. He'd paid his debt to society and lived straight with the law and his neighbors—and himself—for five years now.

The music ended. Their dance was over.

She lifted her head from his shoulder and he released her, his arms dropping to his sides. Better to let go quick. She would never be his to keep. "Beau," she said in a musing tone, "you have the strangest look on your face...."

Nearby, couples broke apart, some of them leaving the floor, others waiting, milling around a little, till the next song began. Still others climbed the steps in pairs from down on the grass.

He said, "I was thinking that we've done okay, you and me...."

She looked at him, real serious, for a second or two, and then she gave him a slow, dazzling smile. "Yeah, and who woulda thought it, huh?"

He chuckled at that and tipped his hat to her. The band started up again, and damn, was he tempted to pull her close for one more dance. But another cowboy stepped in and Beau didn't challenge him.

Starr whirled off in the other man's arms. Beau left the dance floor. He stood watching for a little while and then he turned and headed for his pickup parked in the dirt lot on the other side of the trees.

About a half an hour later, he drove into the yard at the Hart Ranch. The lights were on in the kitchen and living room of the main house.

Beau checked the green-glowing dash clock. Not quite eleven. Not real late, but later than Daniel had said he planned to be up. Beau decided he'd better go on in and check on him before heading for the trailer he called home.

Daniel's dog, Whirlyboy, came off the front porch with a low whine of greeting, his tail wagging hopefully back and forth. "Hey, boy. How's it goin'?" Beau patted the hound's smooth head and Whirlyboy bumped companionably against his leg as Beau climbed the wooden steps to Daniel's front porch.

He paused at the door before he gave it a tap, thinking of Starr again, of her scent that reminded him of jasmine, of her musical laughter on the night air.

Whirlyboy bumped his leg again, eager for a chance to get beyond the door where his master waited.

"We're goin', we're goin'." Beau gave the dog another pat and set his mind to a more constructive subject: the work he had planned for tomorrow. If Daniel was still up, they could take a moment to confer a little. They wanted to move several head of cattle from one pasture, where they'd eaten the grass down, to another where the grass was still long and thick. And, as always, there were fences to check.

True, they didn't need to do a whole lot of conferring on stuff that was already decided. But Beau liked sitting in Daniel's kitchen over a cold drink or a hot cup of coffee, discussing the work ahead, or their plans for the herd. Daniel seemed to enjoy it, too.

Beau tapped on the door. When no answer came, he tapped again, Whirlyboy's tail beating against his leg in anticipation.

Again, there was no answer, just the sound of the dog's impatient panting, an owl hooting out by one of the sheds, the chirping of crickets in the grass—and he thought, from inside, the sound of low voices. Maybe the television in the front room?

Beau turned the knob and pushed open the door. "Daniel?" He stepped into the small entry hall. Whirlyboy slid in around him and headed straight for the front room to the left, disappearing through the open double doors. The lights were on in there and Beau could hear those televised voices droning away. "Daniel?"

No answer, just a sharp spurt of canned laughter. And Whirlyboy, whining in bursts of frustrated sound.

"Daniel?" Beau said a little louder than before.

"In here…" The voice was Daniel's, but tight and low, the words kind of squeezed out around a groan. Beau moved into the doorway—and stopped dead at what he saw.

The worried hound sat whining in canine distress at Daniel's feet, as the big man squirmed in his easy chair.

Daniel's gray face ran sweat, his left hand pressed, clawlike, against his barrel chest. "Think…heart attack…"

No, screamed a frantic voice inside Beau's head.

Not Daniel—no! He'd seen his mother die, and his mean old daddy. One of his brothers was dead, too—Lyle got his in a prison-yard fight. It was enough, Beau thought.

Not Daniel. No way. I won't let him go....

"Just hold on," he told Daniel, his own voice surprising him, it was so level and calm. "I'll get help." Beau spun on his heel for the phone in the hall.

Chapter Two

From the Medicine Creek Clarion,
week of July 10 through July 16

Local Rancher Suffers Heart Attack

Daniel Hart, owner of the Hart Ranch, suffered a heart attack the evening of Friday, July 4. Mr. Hart had been feeling unwell during the day and was discovered by his ranch foreman, Beau Tisdale, in the midst of the attack.

After a swift trip via EMT helicopter to Sheridan, a skilled team of surgeons determined that open-heart surgery was required. "It was touch and go there for a while," reported the foreman when asked for comment. "But he made it through and he'll be okay."

Mr. Hart will be recuperating at Memorial

Hospital in Sheridan "for as long as they make him stay," the foreman said. "He wants to get home the minute they'll let him out of here."

Prayers and good wishes are greatly appreciated.

"Beau's moving into the front bedroom at the house," said Tess. "So he'll be there at night. And they've hired a day nurse to look after Daniel for the first week at home." Tess stood at the counter rolling out pie dough.

Edna, at the stove, slid a heavy crock of beans onto the rack in the oven, pushed the rack in and shut the oven door. "I'm just not sure they should be sending him home." She clucked her tongue, a thoroughly disapproving sound. "Hardly more than a week since that heart attack. And what was that operation he had? A triple bypass?"

"Quintuple," Tess corrected.

"Well, see what I mean? When I had that coronary vasospasm seven years back, they kept *me* up in Sheridan for the same amount of time Daniel is staying there. And what I had wasn't even a true heart attack, let alone the fact that in my case there was no surgery involved."

From her place at the sink cleaning up after breakfast, Starr could see the tiny smile that tugged at Tess's mouth. "Well, now, Edna. Every case is different. And I'd imagine they've made some big strides in medical science in the last seven years. I think we'll just have to trust that the doctors know what they're doing."

"Humph," said Edna and trotted over to the pantry door, vanishing inside.

"Rrrrooom, rrrrooomm." Ethan appeared from the short hall that led to the stairs and the great room. He was flying his favorite plastic jet.

"Ethan," said Tess, "Did you put those blocks in the bin like I told you?"

"Rrrrooom, rrooom, rooommmm..." Ethan kept his jet airborne.

"Ethan John," said his mother, pausing in the process of sprinkling flour on a half-flattened ball of dough. "Stop flying that plane and answer me."

Ethan let his hands drop to his sides, plane and all, and made a big show of slumping his four-and-a-half-year-old shoulders. "Aw, Mommmm..." Tess pointed her rolling pin at him and gave him a narrow-eyed scowl. With a put-upon groan and a tragic expression, Ethan stomped back out the way he'd come.

Edna emerged from the pantry. She held two full Mason jars, one in each hand. "How about blackberry—and this nice apple butter I put up last fall?"

"Perfect," said Tess.

Edna carried the jars to the table and set them down. "So. We'll take the three pies and the beans and the jam over there. What else? We have some of last year's tomatoes...."

As the two older women launched into a discussion of what else should go to the Hart place to welcome Mr. Hart home, Starr wiped up the sink and hung the breakfast pans on their hooks. She poured herself another cup of coffee at about the same time Tess and Edna decided that last year's tomatoes would do just fine. And a couple of loaves of fresh bread, too. Edna would start on the bread right away.

Mug in hand, Starr turned from the coffeemaker and leaned against the counter. ''Who's going to take all this stuff over there?''

Tess carefully guided the flattened dough over a waiting pie. ''Well, we thought we'd do it together, Edna and me.''

Casually, Starr blew across the top of the steaming mug. ''Why don't you let me?'' She dared a hot sip as a thoroughly annoying glance passed between Edna and Tess.

Starr knew they were both thinking about all that mess with Beau in the past. But come on, she was a grown woman now and had a right to make to her own decisions when it came to men—not that there was any decision to be made about Beau. There was nothing between them anymore.

Yeah, she'd danced with him on the Fourth. One dance. And she felt really good inside about that dance. They'd talked like two old friends, and laughed together. When she thought of Beau now, there was no bitterness. All that old garbage was over for good. That dance, to Starr, had signaled true peace between them. She felt really good about that.

But peace between her and Beau didn't mean she meant to run over there and jump the man's bones or anything. Taking the food was a neighborly gesture, and she wanted to do it—and who could say if Beau would even be at the house when she got there?

''Don't you have to work?'' asked Edna.

Starr took a sip of coffee. ''I don't need to go in today.'' Like her employer, she did any and everything over at the *Clarion*—including a little reporting on local goings-on. "I've got a piece for the Ranching Life section to finish up and I have to put together an article on what's going on with the plans for the county fair. I'll do those on my computer and send them over by e-mail. And I can take the opportunity while I'm at the Hart place to do a follow-up on how Mr. Hart's feeling." Jerry had done the original piece, but he'd be pleased if Starr handed in an update. "And besides," she added, "you two have been baking pies and making beans. I'd like to do a little something to help out, too."

"Well," said Edna, still at the table beside the jars of preserves. That was all. Just, *well,* and nothing else.

Tess pinched the edges of her pie and sent Starr a soft smile. "Why not, if you'd like to? That'd be real nice."

Edna's baked beans were the slow-cooking kind. They didn't come out of the oven until four. By then the pies had cooled and the bread was all wrapped and ready to go. They loaded everything into the old Suburban that Zach had bought Tess when they first got married. Starr had inherited the vehicle last year, when Zach bought his wife a new one.

As she was heading off down the long, dusty driveway, one of the ranch pickups came in. Her dad was driving, Jobeth at his side. Starr pulled to the bumpy shoulder so the pickup could get by. Her dad honked and Jobeth waved as they went past. The pickup was covered in mud and so were the two in cab. Starr grinned as she watched the filthy tailgate recede in her rearview mirror. They'd probably been out pulling something large and obstinate from a muddy pond.

It took about twenty-five minutes to get to the Hart place. Starr used a series of back roads made mostly by oil companies drilling test holes, seeking oil-bearing strata. Through the ride, she was aware of a rising feeling of anticipation.

Okay, it was silly. It didn't *mean* anything, but she was really hoping that Beau would be at the house. Maybe they'd talk a little.

The Suburban lurched over a bump in the dirt road and Starr licked her lips and swallowed. She was kind of thirsty. She'd ask for a tall glass of iced tea. If Beau was there, he could keep her company out on Mr. Hart's big front porch while she drank it. Just being neighborly, of course.

And professional. She'd interview Beau on Mr. Hart's convalescence while she sipped that cool, refreshing tea.

Beau was standing on the porch, staring off into nowhere, trying pretty much unsuccessfully to get his mind around the enormity of what Daniel had just told him, when he spotted Tess's old Suburban coming up the drive.

For a moment or two, he just stared, his mind still back there in the bedroom, hearing, but hardly daring to believe, the things Daniel was saying to him. And then, as the vehicle drew closer, he frowned. He hadn't seen Tess driving it since Zach bought her the new one....

In fact, hadn't Zach said they'd passed the old one to Starr for her use whenever she was home?

Beau straightened from the post he'd been leaning

against. With the wild mustangs on the loose in his chest again, he stuck his hands in his side pockets and waited for the Suburban to pull to a stop about ten feet from the base of the porch steps.

Starr beamed him a smile through her side window. The mustangs bucked high and his breath snagged hard in his throat. The window slid down and she stuck her head out. That midnight hair, loose around her angel face, caught the sun and gave off a blue-black shine.

"Hey, Beau."

Dazzled, he gulped to make his throat relax. "Hey."

"How's Mr. Hart?"

"Doing well. Real well. Chomping at the bit to get out of bed and back to work."

"I heard you hired him a nurse."

"Yeah. He's already making the poor woman crazy with his demands to be up and about."

"Hope she's strong enough to make him stay in that bed until he's well enough to get out of it."

"You know Althea Hecht?" The nurse, a local woman, stood about five-eleven and weighed a hundred and eighty or so pounds, very little of it fat.

Starr was nodding. "Althea can keep him in line if anyone can—and I've got a Suburban full of food. Pies and Edna's baked beans, fresh-baked bread and half a pantry's worth of preserves."

He came down the steps, his boots seeming to him like they barely skimmed the old boards. "My stomach is already growling."

"Come on, then." She leaned on her door. It swung

open and she jumped lightly to the ground. "Help me get it all inside."

He followed her around to the hatch in back, noticing the little spiral-top notebook and the pen she had stuck in a back pocket, but more interested in the way her womanly hips swayed as she walked, in that gleaming waterfall of shining raven hair.

Today was stacking up to be pretty nigh on perfect. Daniel Hart had called him the son he'd never had.

And Starr Bravo was right there in front of him, close enough to reach out and touch.

Beau led Starr into the house and signaled the way back to the kitchen. He fell in step behind her, where he could admire the sway of her hips a little more. Coming or going, Starr Bravo was a pleasure to look at.

They found Althea in the kitchen. She was brewing decaf for Daniel. The nurse and Starr greeted each other. Althea sighed over the scent of Tess's pies and groused in a good-natured way over her patient's orneriness.

"'Real coffee, damn it,' he growls at me. 'Real coffee, strong and black.' Well, I didn't even bother to inform him that decaf is the closest he's getting to real coffee while he's in my care...."

Starr laughed, the sound making the dim old kitchen seem sunny and bright, as if someone had knocked out a wall and the warm daylight outside had come streaming in to push back every shadow, to fill every corner with golden light. "Althea, we know you can handle him."

Althea grunted. "You got that right. I give my patients the best care there is, no matter how hard *some* of them try to keep me from doing it.''

Starr asked, "I wonder if could step in and say hello."

Althea poured the coffee. "Don't see why not."

Daniel was propped up on his pillows, looking grouchy, when they entered. He'd let Whirlyboy in to lie on a rag rug in the corner. At the sight of Starr, the dog thumped his tail. The old man's scowl lightened to a grin. "Well, if it isn't Starr Bravo. How you been, girl?"

"I've been just fine." She went over and gave Whirlyboy a scratch behind the ear. "Home for my last summer and enjoying every minute of it. But what about you, Mr. Hart?"

Daniel made a low noise in his throat and his scowl returned—directed at Althea, who was easing the bed tray across his lap. "Better than some people would have you believe." The nurse got the coffee from where she'd set it on the bed stand and handed it over. He sniffed it suspiciously. "Not strong enough. I can tell by the smell of it, by the watery way it sloshes in the mug."

"It's all you're getting," Althea informed him with exaggerated sweetness. "I suggest you enjoy it."

Daniel slurped and grumbled some more. "It's not bad enough I'm a prisoner in my own bed. I can't even get a decent cup of coffee anymore." He set the cup down and winked at Beau. Beau gave him a nod in return and Daniel smiled at Starr. "But even if the coffee's bad, a pretty girl is always welcome. Brightens my day and that is a certainty."

Starr gave him a modest smile and told him her family had sent pies and some other things.

"I thank you," Daniel replied with a regal nod of his big, nearly bald head. "I always did appreciate Edna's slow-cooked beans. And there are no words to describe those pies of Tess's. Pass my thanks to both of them, will you please?"

"I'll do that. And the word is you'll be on your feet again real soon."

"That's right." He sent Althea another look. "*Real* soon."

They spoke for a few minutes more—of the weather, which was mild, of the alfalfa crop, which looked like a good one this year. And, as always, about beef prices, which had been better, but could be worse.

As Beau led her from the room, Daniel urged her to come back and visit anytime. Starr paused in the doorway to promise she'd be around to check on him again soon. Beau felt his ears prick up when she said that. With a little luck, he might be there at the house the next time she came by.

"You'd better do what Althea tells you," she warned in a teasing way.

Daniel snorted. "Can't see as how I have any choice."

She turned to Beau and he led her through the hall and around through the front room, on the way to the door. She spoke before they reached the entry hall. "Beau?" He stopped and turned, pleasure running in a warm current all through him, that she was here in the place where he lived, saying his name in a friendly, hopeful tone. "I went off without the cooler. I'm a little thirsty. A cold drink would be so nice...."

Damn. He'd never even thought to offer her something. "I'm sorry."

She was looking right at him. And that warm current inside him was going molten hot. "Nothing to be sorry about. Iced tea, maybe?"

He led her back to the kitchen and poured her the cold tea.

"Thanks. Maybe you'll sit out on the porch with me while I drink this?"

"Be glad to."

As soon as they got out there, before they even had a chance to sit down, she was pointing to the stand of cottonwoods and willows fifty yards or so away on the north side of the house. "Is that a creek over there?"

He had his hat, collected from the rack by the door on the way out. He beat it lightly against his thigh and slid it onto his head. "More like a big ditch. Feeds into the pond in the back pasture."

She sipped from the tall, already sweat-frosted glass. "Umm. This is just what I needed. Thank you."

"Welcome." He looked at her soft red mouth. He could still recall, like it was yesterday, the tender, hungry feel of that mouth under his. She had the longest, blackest eyelashes of any woman he'd ever seen. He watched as they swept down and then up again.

"It's a nice day," she remarked. "A little hot." Oh, yeah, he thought. *Hot.* That's the right word. "We could just stroll on over there—to that ditch, I mean. I'll bet it's cool under the trees."

"Sure."

She wore Wranglers and good, serviceable boots

and a plain white shirt with short sleeves, tucked in. No slice of bare belly to tempt him today. Once, in one of their brief stolen times together, she'd confessed she had one of those navel rings—and a tattoo in a place where only the right man was ever going to see it.

The other night, he hadn't noticed any navel ring. Maybe she didn't wear it anymore.

Then again, he hadn't caught a glimpse of her navel, now had he? That red, one-shoulder shirt had stayed low enough to safely shield it from his hungry eyes.

She was halfway down the steps. He needed no encouragement to follow.

In the trees, it was cool, just as she'd predicted. They sat on the grassy slope that led down to the cheerfully bubbling stream and she sipped her tea. "Nice," she said with happy sigh.

He leaned back on an elbow, picked a small blue flower that grew in the grass, and twirled it by the stem for a second or two before tossing it out into the rushing water. It bobbed away, a spot of blue, until the current sucked it under.

She said, "Oh, I almost forgot…" The ice cubes clinked in her half-empty glass as she found a level place to set it. She reached into her back pocket and came out with that notebook and pen he'd seen earlier. "I was hoping to get a few quotes from you about how Mr. Hart's recovery is progressing."

"For the *Clarion?*"

"Uh-huh." She flipped open the notebook, held her pen poised.

He grinned. "Quotes from the *foreman?*"

She was close enough to reach out and give his arm

a tap with that pen. "Well, you are Mr. Hart's top hand, aren't you?"

"Considering I'm his *only* full-time, year-round hand, I guess saying I'm top hand wouldn't be that far wrong." He watched her silky black lashes sweep down and up again. Then he challenged, "It was you, wasn't it—you told Jerry Esponda to put me down as Daniel's foreman?"

She stuck out her chin at him. "So what if I did? Are you demanding a retraction?"

He leaned just a fraction closer to her and got an intoxicating whiff of jasmine for his pains. "I'm demanding nothing. You can relax."

She leaned closer still. "That is such a relief...."

He looked from her eyes to her mouth and back again. She was doing it, too—that violet gaze tracking: Eyes. Lips. Eyes. Lips…

He wanted to kiss her so bad that his need had a taste—like honey, but with a bitter edge.

There had been other women in his life. Not that many. A few. He was a man, after all. But no matter how many other women he flirted with or kissed or took to bed, there would always be this woman, somewhere back in a yearning, hopeful corner of his heart.

Beau knew what he was, and what he would never be. Yet somehow, inevitably, in the last moments of loving, when need swallowed him whole, he would close his eyes and see Starr's face.

Carefully, he canted back away from her. With mingled regret and relief, he watched her do the same.

She sat up straight and made a few scratches at the pad with her pen. "So. He's recovering quickly…"

Beau found another flower, picked it, twirled it,

tossed it away. "Yeah. He'd be out stringing fence right now if Althea wasn't holding him down."

"Hmm. May I quote you on that?"

He gave a snort of laughter. "'Recovering quickly' sounds better, I think—and you know, you surprised the heck outta me when you came rolling up in that old Suburban."

She granted him a pert glance. "I happen to love that SUV."

"What about that little sports car you used to drive way back when?"

Something changed in her face. Maybe she was remembering the bold-seeming, unhappy girl she'd been once. "Sold it. It wasn't much use in a Wyoming winter—let alone against all the ruts in the dirt roads on the Rising Sun." Her expression went teasing again. "And is that all you have to tell me about Mr. Hart's improving health?"

"That is the sum total of what I have to report. *'Mr. Hart is recovering quickly,' ranch foreman Beau Tisdale said.* Put that in the paper—and you can add that bit about prayers and good wishes. Those never hurt."

"Hah. So you did like being called the foreman."

What he liked was the sound of her voice, the jasmine scent of her, the way the dapples of sun made blue lights in her hair. "Yeah," he said, his voice a little huskier than he should have allowed it to be. "I liked it fine. And it didn't seem to bother Daniel any when he saw it in the paper." He'd been a little nervous that Daniel would assume *he'd* told Jerry he was ranch foreman, that Daniel might think he'd overstepped himself. But that was yesterday, when the

Clarion came out. Yesterday he hadn't understood the extent of Daniel's regard for him.

Hell. He still wasn't sure he could believe what Daniel had said an hour ago....

"First of all, I need to tell you now, so the chance doesn't slip away from me, that you are the son I never had...."

"Beau?" Starr was looking at him sideways, a soft smile on that unforgettable mouth. He cocked an eyebrow at her. Her smile widened. "What's on your mind? You got the funniest look just now."

Damned if he didn't want to tell her. Strange. He wasn't a man who shared his triumphs—or his hurts. But it was all so new. It almost didn't seem real.

And he found that he wanted to talk about it, to say right out how his life was so suddenly and unbelievably changed. It would make it more real, to tell someone.

Not just anyone, though.

He wanted to tell Starr and only Starr. In a way, it was like some dream, that she was here now, at this moment, so soon after Daniel had told him.

It was also like a dream that all the old bad feelings between them seemed gone at last, that he was talking to her so casually, like they were good friends. Six years ago, it had amazed him how easy she was to talk to. And here she was after all this time and that ease between them was back, like it had always been there, waiting for her to understand and forgive him for what he'd done that day in the yard at the Rising Sun....

"Beau?" She was looking at him so hopefully. She wanted to hear whatever he had on his mind.

He kind of edged into it, giving her a grin. "You got to promise you won't go putting it in the paper...."

She blinked. "Well, yeah. Sure." She kind of frowned and smiled at the same time. "What? Beau, what is it?"

"Just, you know, between you and me..."

"Of course, if you want it that way."

"Yeah. I do. It's not something the whole county needs to know." There would be talk, when it came out. He was not blood kin to Daniel. He'd been in prison. And his name was Tisdale. In Medicine Creek, most anyone could tell you that the Tisdales were no good. A lot of folks would disbelieve—and disapprove—when they heard. But that wouldn't be for years yet. Daniel was going to pull through just fine. And Beau planned to see that the older man took care of himself, just like a real son would.

"I will not tell a soul," she vowed.

So he said it. "Today Daniel told me that he's leaving the ranch to me." He sat up, hooked an elbow on either knee and looked at the clear, sparkling stream for a moment. Then he slanted a glance at Starr. "I gotta tell you, I'm having some trouble believing it's true."

"Oh, Beau..." Her voice trailed off. Her face seemed to glow. She looked so happy. Happy for *him*.

He grunted. "Pretty hard to believe, huh?"

She gave him a firm shake of her head. "No. No, it isn't. Not hard to believe at all. But very good news. And, well, kind of *right*, you know?"

"You think so?" His own voice surprised him. He sounded just like he felt—young. Hopeful as a kid at

Christmas. He'd learned early in his life that it didn't pay to let anyone know how you felt.

But this was Starr he was telling. From the first, he'd found it way too easy to show her what was going on inside him.

Now she was nodding. "Oh, yeah. I do think so. My dad's always saying how hard you work for Mr. Hart. And how great it's turned out, him taking you on."

"Zach's been real good to me, too. I'm grateful."

"So is Mr. Hart, don't you think? I mean, that you came along. After all, he's got no blood family left. And now, it's kind of like *you're* his family, isn't it?"

"Yeah," he said, still marveling at the way it all worked out. "That's how I feel about it. It truly is...."

She reached across the small distance between them and laid her soft hand on his arm. A warm glow seemed to radiate from the place where she touched him. The wind whispered through the trees and the cottonwood fluff blew around in the air and the warm sun glinted off the rushing stream.

Eventually, she let go, but it seemed to Beau that he could still feel the warm clasp of her hand. With a small, contented sigh, she stretched out on the grass and laced her fingers behind her head. She stared up at the fluttering leaves of the cottonwood that sheltered them—and beyond, to the wide, blue sky overhead.

Beau set his hat aside and stretched out beside her. For a while, they just lay there, watching the leaves above move in the wind, listening to the happy, bubbly sound of the stream at their feet and the occasional soft coo of a mourning dove somewhere nearby.

"Beau?" He turned from the view of the trees and

the sky to meet her waiting eyes. She looked thoughtful and maybe a little bit anxious. "There's been
something I've been wishing I could ask you for a few
years now."

He had a pretty good idea where she was headed.
"So ask."

He watched her smooth throat move as she swallowed. "That day Tess caught us in the barn together,
those horrible things you said to me out in the yard…"

"Yeah?"

"Did you mean them?"

Beau lay still, one hand on his stomach, the other
cradling his head. She shifted, turning toward him on
her side, propping her head on her hand. All that black
hair spilled over her palm and fell along her arm to
kiss the green, green grass.

"Well…" Her mouth trembled a little. "Did you?"

"No," he said softly. "I didn't mean those things
I said. Those things were lies, pure and simple." He
felt the pained smile as it twisted his mouth. "And I
put a lot of effort into being a convincing enough rat-
bastard that you would think they were true."

She let out a long sigh, as if she'd been holding her
breath and just remembered to let it out. "I knew it.
But I did want to hear you say it—just like I want to
hear you tell me *why* you said those things…"

"Hell," he replied, as if that was any kind of answer. All these years he'd nursed a hopeless yearning
that someday they'd talk about this. Someday when
she was a grown woman and he'd come through the
bad things he'd done, come through to make himself
another, better kind of life. And today, here they were,

and it was happening just the way he'd always dreamed it might....

One hell of a day, this one. The day Daniel said he considered Beau as his son. The day Starr showed up with offerings of food from her family—and now seemed reluctant to leave.

He said, "I only knew then that I was headed for a bad place and I had to make sure you didn't try to follow me there."

"Oh," she said so softly, the way a woman might exclaim upon unwrapping some beautiful and priceless gift. And then she called it exactly that—a gift. "Life is so strange, isn't it?" she whispered, a certain reverence in her low voice. "I mean, what you did was so brave, really. It turned out to be like a...gift. It hurt so damn much when you did it, but my life turned out different—so much better than the direction I was headed in then, because you said those awful things to me, because they made me think, and think hard, about my life. Made me reach out to my family. Made me see I had to make some changes, or I could end up..." She didn't seem to know how to finish.

So he did it for her. "...following the wrong guy down the road to nowhere and never finding your way back?"

Tears welled in her eyes, making them shine all the brighter. She didn't let him see them fall, but sat up, quickly, turning away. Touched in the deepest part of himself, he left her alone until she could get it together.

Finally, she turned to him again, her eyes still suspiciously shiny-looking, but her soft cheeks dry. "Yeah. Yeah, I guess that's it. But look." She raised her hands, palms up, as if to include everything—the rushing water, the summer sky, the trees whispering in the warm wind—even the faint cooing of that lone mourning dove. "I didn't go down that road. And you…well, Beau. You have done it. You've found your way back."

Chapter Three

For a while, they just sat there, side by side, staring off toward the stream and the open pasture that rolled away from them beyond the trees on the other side. Eventually, she picked up her tea, drained the last of it and tossed the remaining melted slivers of ice out into the water.

He put on his hat and got up, holding down a hand. She took it, tugging on it lightly as she rose. He felt a much stronger tug, down inside him—an ache for what might have been, if only he were someone that he would never be. Once she was on her feet, he made himself let go.

They hesitated, facing each other there on the bank, both knowing they should turn for the house, but neither making a move.

"Back then, all those years ago," she said softly,

"I'd never felt…oh, I don't know. Accepted, I guess. I'd never felt accepted, or at home, with anyone. Not until I met you. For that short time we had, I felt I could tell you anything and you would understand. That you wouldn't judge me, that you knew who I really was, deep down. And that you liked that person."

"I did like that person." The words came out before he even realized he would say them. "I liked that person a whole hell of a lot. I still do."

Her smile was so shy. It trembled at the edges. "I'm glad to hear that. And you know, today, after so much time has gone by…I feel just the same. That I could sit right back down in the grass again with you and we could talk forever. That I could tell you everything that's in my most secret heart and know I was telling it all to someone I can trust. I don't think I want to give that up right now, Beau. Not when I've just found it again." She bit her still-quivering lip to make it be still. "I guess what I'm getting at is…do you think that we might…?" Her words trailed off, but he knew where she was headed.

And it was impossible. "Starr—"

"Oh, wait," she cried. "Can't I finish?"

He stuck his hands in his pockets to keep them from doing something they shouldn't. "Go ahead."

"Well, it's just…" She looked down into her empty glass, then up at him again. "I do know we're going in different directions now. And I haven't forgotten the things you said once. That all you wanted in life was a real home and a chance to work hard every day building something that was your own. Against all the odds, you've got what you wanted. And I'm off to

New York in the fall, to start a new job. In a few months, I'm gone. Off to live the life I've been studying and planning for. I'm not saying either of us should change, or start thinking about giving up the lives we've worked hard to make. I'm not really talking about anything permanent. I'm just saying that, well, there's a whole summer stretching out ahead of us. Why couldn't we spend a little time together, now and then, before I go?''

''Be...friends, you mean?''

''Yeah,'' she said. ''Friends. That's what I mean.''

How could she ask for that? She had to know it would never work. He couldn't even stand next to her on Daniel's porch without wondering if she still had that navel ring, without wanting to grab her and kiss her—and to maybe get his chance to see that secret tattoo.

But she was so sweetly, adorably hopeful, so damned impossibly beautiful as she stood there in front of him, asking him why they couldn't just be summertime friends. He didn't have the heart—let alone the will—to say no.

And why the hell *should* he say no, a darker voice down inside him was whispering? Why shouldn't he see her if she wanted to see him? He was a straight-ahead guy now, an upstanding citizen who put in an honest day's work for his pay.

He might not be the right guy for her in the long run, but she wasn't sixteen anymore. She was all grown up, old enough to make a woman's decisions. Who said he had to deny himself her company, if she wanted to share it with him?

Because it'll break your damn heart to see her go,

fool, whispered another voice, a wiser one, in the back of his mind. *It'll break your damn heart—and just possibly hers, as well.*

He found he was having a hell of a time trying to listen to that wiser voice. How could he do it? How could he say no when she stood right there, close enough to touch, gleaming black hair stirring in the wind, asking him so sweetly and sincerely to be allowed to see him now and then?

"Tell you what."

She laughed. "You look so serious."

This is *serious, damn it,* he thought. *What'll we get but heartbreak, if we start this thing between us all over again?* He said, "Think it over."

Those silky brows drew together. "But it's not a big deal. It's only—"

He shook his head to silence her. It *was* a big deal, whether she was willing to admit it or not. "Think it over. Be real sure you want to get something started with me again—even just for the summer."

"But Beau, I already told you. I do want to see you again. Now, whether I'd call that 'getting something started—'"

"Call it whatever you damn well please." She flinched and he realized he'd spoken too harshly. He gentled his tone. "I just want you to give it some thought before we start up with anything."

"But..." She looked enchantingly bewildered. "Do *you* want to spend more time with *me?*"

Do bears like honey? He confessed, "Yeah. Yeah, I'd like that. I'd like it a lot."

"Well, then..." A few strands of hair had got caught across her mouth. He kept his hands shoved hard in his pockets to keep from reaching out and smoothing those strands back over her soft cheek, behind the graceful curve of her ear. After a few seconds that seemed like a year, she brushed them away herself.

"Think about it," he said, his heart pounding deep and hard, every beat seeming to call out her name. "Give it week. By next Friday, if you still think you want to go out with me, you give me a call."

Those lashes swept down. "I know my own mind, Beau."

"We'll see."

She looked straight at him then, violet eyes flashing with irritation. "I'm not asking for a lifetime. Just the summer. Just a chance to be together, now and then, for a little while…"

"And all *I'm* asking is that you give it some thought first."

Her eyes went wide and she fell back a step. "Do you remember? You said almost the exact same words before you kissed me the first time?"

He did remember. They were in the tack room, off the barn at the Rising Sun. They'd been talking— about the wild stuff she'd done down in San Diego, about how he'd never been much farther than Cheyenne himself, except for that one trip to Arkansas with his mom all those years and years ago. He was leaning on a saddle horn. She slid right up close to him and lifted her mouth.

"Give it some thought," he'd said. *"Before you go offering up those sweet lips of yours…"*

Yeah, he remembered. He remembered all of it— every magical, forbidden moment with her.

He said it once more. "Give it some thought."

She turned her head away from him then, abruptly, black hair flying out. It took her a moment before she faced him again. "You are impossible sometimes, you know that? I *have* thought about it. I've thought about it all I need to. By next Friday, I'll feel just the same."

"Then next Friday, you'll be giving me a call." A wry smile pulled at the edges of his mouth. "And could we maybe not argue about this anymore?"

She folded her arms tight under those tempting full breasts of hers. "You're like an old mule sometimes, you know that?"

"All your flattering words will get you exactly nowhere with me."

She laughed, then. He drank in the sound. "Oh, all right. Have it your way." She sent him a sideways look. "And expect a call from me. Friday."

"I'll be right here. I'm not goin' anywhere."

Starr knew what she wanted—one sweet final summer at home that would include Beau—and what she wanted was not going to change. She knew very well that Beau wanted the same thing. She'd seen it in those sky-blue eyes of his. He'd even said so when she asked him.

So what was his problem? Why was he putting her off? The summer wasn't going to last forever, after all. It was already almost the middle of July. Why waste a whole week when she'd told him there was no reason to?

She didn't have to think all that hard to come up with the answer: Because he wanted her to be sure. Because he cared for her. Because he'd *always* cared.

She drove home over the rutted dirt roads, alternately grinning and scowling, rehearsing the clever, teasing things she'd say to him when the long week ahead finally ended and she had his permission to give him a call.

The weekend seemed to crawl by. It took forever and a year to get from Saturday to Sunday. Sunday night lasted a lifetime and a half.

Then came Monday. She got up and ate her breakfast, already wishing the day would hurry up and end.

She spent the morning at the paper, and headed home at lunch. Late Monday afternoon, she was up in her room finishing up the article about the county fair. She clicked on Copy, shoving back her chair to get up and stretch—and just happening to glance out the window at the exact moment the green pickup drove in.

It rolled on past the barn and pulled to a stop by one of the sheds.

Starr shot out the bedroom door and raced down the stairs so fast, she almost plowed into Edna in the central hall.

Edna let out a shriek and staggered back.

Starr caught her by her dainty little shoulders. "Oops. Sorry…" She guided the older woman to the side and flew on by.

"What *is* the all-fired hurry?" Edna grumbled from behind her.

Starr tore into the kitchen, grabbed a glass from the cupboard, stuck it under the ice dispenser in the door of the fridge and tapped a toe in impatience as the cubes tumbled out much too slowly for her liking. When the ice was finally in there, she slammed the glass on the counter, threw open the fridge door and grabbed the big jar of cold tea that Tess always kept full during the warm months. Somehow, she managed to slosh it into the glass without spilling a drop.

"Sugar?" she muttered under her breath. Did he like sugar? It bothered her no end that she didn't even know.

Well, no time for that now. He'd too likely be gone if she didn't get out there.

Abandoning the open jar of tea on the counter, she spun for the back door, vaguely aware that Tess was sitting at the table with Ethan while he ate a snack and Edna had appeared in the doorway to the hall. They all three stared at her as if she'd lost her mind.

"Tea." She beamed at the three gaping faces and held the glass high. "For Beau..." Whirling, she raced out through the combination laundry and mud-room, not caring in the least that she let the screen slam behind her.

The pickup was still there and Beau was unloading stuff from the bed. She slowed to a more dignified stroll until she reached him, at which point he granted her a quick tip of his hat. After that, she stood back, waiting, until he'd finished what he'd come to do. Once the last piece of equipment was stowed in the shed, he came striding on over to her, faded shirt dark with sweat in a V down his chest and beneath his strong arms, hat and boots dusty.

Something tightened down inside her, just to look at him. And her breath, for a second or two, kind of stalled out in her throat. She put on her most uncon-cerned expression. "Thought you might like a cool glass of tea after all the heavy lifting."

He looked her up and down. She wore old jeans,

ragged running shoes and a baggy C.U. T-shirt, but the way his gaze went over her made her feel like the most gorgeous and glamorous thing around. "I do appreciate a nice, cold drink."

"I realized I have no idea if you take sugar or not?"

"With or without, it's fine with me. I'm easy to please."

"Well. Fine, then." She handed it over.

He tipped his head back and drank it down in one long swallow. "Thank you." His fingers brushed hers as he handed back the glass. A shiver of pleasure went through her, just from that slight, too-brief touch. "Gotta get a move on," he said. "Tell your dad I was here, that I put everything in the shed?"

"Be happy to."

He hitched up the tailgate and turned for the driver's door. She trailed along after, longing to ask him to stick around for a while, but mindful of the agreement she'd reluctantly struck with him.

Not until Friday…

He climbed in and pulled the door shut, then leaned out the window. "See you later." His eyes said a lot more than his mouth did. He scanned her face as if he couldn't get enough of looking at her.

"Friday," she told him firmly, just so he'd know she had not changed her mind. "You'll be seeing me Friday."

For that, she got one of those slow smiles of his. "Number's in the book."

"I know. I checked—and how's Mr. Hart doing?"

"Ornerier every day." He turned on the engine, gunned it just a little, and rolled on away from her, resting his elbow on the window frame, waving as he went.

"Friday," she promised under her breath, waving back, as the pickup disappeared around the front of the house. She looked into the drained glass of ice cubes. "Or maybe, Beau Tisdale, sooner than that…"

In the kitchen, Tess and Ethan were still at the table. Edna stood at the counter, chopping onions with a big knife and sniffing delicately to hold back the tears. Some thoughtful person had already recapped the tea and put it away. Starr beamed them all a huge, happy smile. She tossed the ice cubes in the sink and stuck the glass in the dishwasher. Then she marched into the pantry, emerging a few moments later with twin canisters—one containing superfine flour, the other sugar—and a box of baking chocolate squares.

She got the big mixing bowl from a low cabinet, brought down the stained red-and-white covered *Better Homes and Gardens* cookbook and set it all on a section of counter out of Edna's way.

Edna sniffed. "A sudden burning need to bake?"

"As a matter of fact, yes." Starr pulled open the fridge and took out three eggs and a cube of butter. "I just know Mr. Hart would love a nice chocolate-layer cake."

At eight-thirty that evening, as Starr pulled into the yard at the Hart Ranch, the big, red ball of the sun was sinking behind the Bighorn Mountains. She got out and went around for the Tupperware cake carrier, taking it by the handle and marching right up the steps to the front door.

Mr. Hart himself answered her knock. "Well, hello, Starr."

"Mr. Hart. You're lookin' good."

He leaned a little closer. "Tell that to Althea—and I think you're about grown up enough to start calling me by my given name."

"I'll do that, then. Daniel." She forced herself not to crane around his looming frame to see if Beau just might be standing behind him in the hall.

"Come on in." He stepped back so she could get by him.

In the kitchen, that friendly hound she remembered from the other day lay on his rag rug in the corner. He beat his tail on the floor in greeting. Beau was sitting at the table nursing a beer. He stood briefly when she entered.

"Hi, Beau." She gave him a quick nod, as if his being there were merely incidental to her purpose in coming. She thought she sounded pretty cool and collected, especially considering that fluttery creatures had taken flight in her stomach and her pulse beat faster just at the sight of him. "Where's Althea?"

"She goes home at six." Beau's voice was real casual, but his eyes drank her in. He settled back into his chair, facing out from the table, his long legs in an easy sprawl. "She needs a little rest at home after all day dealing with that one there." He pointed his beer at Daniel.

Daniel grunted. "She'll get all the rest she needs soon enough. My days of requiring a nurse are numbered—and what's inside that Tupperware? Looks to me like that might be a cake."

She set it on the table, brushing Beau's denim-clad knee in the process—completely by accident, of course. "Chocolate. Baked it myself."

"Starr, you have read the mind of this old man. Chocolate's my favorite."

"It's a little lopsided," she confessed, all modesty. "But the flavor's the same. And I used dark chocolate. I hear it's good for your heart."

"I will enjoy it, I can promise you that." He gestured at Beau with a flick of his balding head. "I'll even share it with Althea and this one here—if the two of 'em treat me right, that is."

Beau raised his beer to Daniel before taking a sip.

"Sit down, sit down," said Daniel, crossing around behind Beau and pulling out a chair for her.

She looked at Beau, whose eyes seemed to eat her up—at the same time as they warned her to remember their agreement. She cleared her throat. "Uh, no. Really. It'll be dark soon. I should get home…"

Beau set down his beer. "I'll walk you out."

"Why, thank you, Beau."

On the porch, she hung back. Yeah, okay. She was behaving shamelessly. But with Beau, being shameless was just so much fun. "How 'bout a walk down by that little stream again?"

In the fading daylight, his smile was slow, his gaze watchful. "How 'bout you remember what we agreed?"

She resisted the urge to remind him that it hadn't been any real kind of agreement. He'd said how it was going to be and refused to give her the slightest chance to persuade him otherwise. "Well," she said sweetly, "I guess I'll be going then."

She slid around him and went on down the steps. When she reached the Suburban, his hand came around her and opened the door. "Why, thank you,

Beau,'' she said again in the same tone she'd used in the house, all sweetness and light.

''My pleasure.''

She climbed up onto the seat and he shut the door. ''See you….''

'''Bye, Starr.''

She felt kind of sad as she drove away—sad and a little let down. She'd wanted more from the visit. But then she looked in her rearview mirror when she was halfway down the driveway, just before the big curve. Beau was still standing there, watching her go.

''Till Friday,'' she whispered to the tall, broad-shouldered shape of him against the darkening sky. ''Till Friday…''

Chapter Four

Starr turned on the bedside lamp and looked at her alarm clock. "Yes!" she announced with enthusiasm to her empty bedroom.

She shoved back the sheet and grabbed the phone, dialing the number without having to look it up. She had it memorized—no, more than just memorized. It was burned into her brain.

He answered before the second ring. "Hart Ranch."

"I knew you'd be up."

He didn't say anything for a moment. She enjoyed the silence, the awareness that he was there, on the other end of the line. "It's the middle of the night," he reminded her at last.

"Twelve-o-three," she announced with glee. "Twelve-o-three on *Friday* morning, to be specific."

He grunted. "You know, Daniel might have answered. What would you have said then?"

"'May I please speak to Beau?'"

"Pretty sure of yourself, aren't you?" The warmth in his voice told her she had no reason not to be.

"So." She heaved a happy sigh. "Where shall we go for our first date tonight?"

"Got it all planned out, huh?"

She flopped back on the pillows and stared dreamily at the ceiling. "Well, not *all* of it. As I just said, there's still the question of where we should go...."

"Let me know when you make up your mind."

She forked her fingers back through her sleep-tangled hair and considered. "How about Arlington's?" The steak house was one of the three nice dinner houses in Medicine Creek. "Or the Stagecoach Grill—or Carmelita's."

"I take it we're going out to eat?"

"Is that an objection?"

"Starr..." Something in his voice made her clutch the phone a little tighter.

"Yeah?"

"Your dad know you're on the phone with me in the middle of the night, discussing which restaurant we'll go to tonight?"

Irritation stabbed at her. "Come on. I'm over twenty-one. My dad knows *that*. And Beau?"

"What?" he said reluctantly.

"This isn't six years ago. I'm not telling anyone any lies. I want to go out with you and I'll say it straight out to anyone who asks."

"I'd better have a word with him."

She huffed out a hard breath. "You do not have to ask my dad if you can go out with me."

"I don't intend to ask him. I'll *tell* him, respectfully.

Your dad's done more for me than I can ever repay. It's the least I can do to tell him ahead of time that you and me will be spending some time together.''

She hauled herself up against the headboard again. ''I have a better idea.'' He made a low, sort of doubtful sound. ''Don't knock it till you've heard it—how's Daniel doing?''

''He's up and about. Taking it easy, though. Yesterday he got up with me and insisted on helping with the horses and the two bum calves we're keeping out in back of the barn. And today will be Althea's last day.'' He added, wariness creeping in, ''Why?''

''Come to dinner, here, tonight. Both you and Daniel. Everyone would be glad to have you. And it can be a kind of celebration, that Daniel's feeling better. We'll feed the hands early and eat in the dining room. Edna loves to break out the good tablecloth and the nice china. And during the evening we'll just mention, real casually, that you and I will be going out tomorrow night.''

A moment passed while he thought that over. ''Like I said. Got it all figured out, haven't you?'' His voice was so soft, thrillingly intimate.

She asked, huskiness creeping in, ''Do you have a problem with that?''

''What if I do?''

''Then get over it. And be here at six.''

Starr took the silver filigree ring from her napkin and smoothed the napkin on her lap. She caught Beau's eye across the table and a sweet feeling of anticipation shivered through her.

At the end of the table, her dad bowed his head.

Starr bowed hers, too. After a few words of thanks, they began passing the steaming bowls of food and the big platter of perfectly seared Rising Sun T-bones.

"I have to admit, these are just beautiful," Edna remarked as she forked up a steak and laid it on her plate. When they'd planned the menu, Edna had suggested chicken—lower cholesterol and less fat. But both Starr and Tess had argued that this was a special occasion and Daniel did deserve to have his beef now and then.

Judging by Daniel's big smile when he saw those steaks, they'd made the right choice. Starr thought the sweet old guy looked pretty good in the light of the tall white candles Edna had placed in heirloom silver candlesticks in the middle of the table. His broad, jowly face, kind of pale that first day he got home, had better color now.

The dinner went well, the talk flowing easily, punctuated with bursts of shared laughter. The men discussed the usual: which cattle should be moved where, what fences needed repair. Jobeth described her latest 4-H project. Ethan ate his meal quietly and for once hardly squirmed at all.

Starr traded endless knowing glances with Beau. Each separate shared look warmed her all the way down to her toes. With all that excitement buzzing inside her, it was hard to act casual.

Too bad that, somehow, the moment to mention their plans for tomorrow just never seemed to come. Maybe, she decided near the end of the meal, announcing it at dinner wasn't such a great idea, anyway. There'd be all those meaningful looks Tess and Edna would share. And probably a snicker or two from Jo-beth. And who could predict how her dad would react?

So really, why go there? Who she dated was her business. If Beau thought he had to say something to her dad, he could just go ahead and do it on his own.

By then, the glances Beau gave her had become questioning ones. Instead of meeting his eyes, she started letting her gaze kind of slide away. She paid a lot of attention to her water glass and to eating the last glazed carrot on her plate.

Finally, during a slight lull in the conversation, Beau spoke up. "So Starr. Did you decide where you want to go to dinner tomorrow night?"

The lull kind of opened up into something that just might have been called a deathly silence. Starr looked up from her carrot and saw the glances go shooting back and forth between Edna and Tess. Jobeth snick-ered.

And then her dad said, "Arlington's is good. But I think the Grill is better."

Beau arrived in the old bench-seat style green pickup at six-thirty the next evening. He had the ve-hicle shiny clean and ready for a night on the town.

They took her dad's suggestion and went to the Stagecoach Grill, where the tables had royal-blue cloths on them and a west-facing picture window framed a spectacular view of the Bighorns, the clouds that snagged on the crests turning purple as the day began to fade.

"You talked to my dad ahead of time," she accused after the waitress had taken their order.

He leaned back in his chair and grinned at her. "I

thought it was a bad idea to spring it on the poor guy in the middle of dinner like that. So yeah, I had a word with him earlier in the day.''

"Well, you could have just told me so.''

"You can be a hard woman to get through to sometimes, you know?''

She fiddled with her water glass and kind of screwed up her mouth at him, thinking of how he'd made her wait all last week. "Oh, yeah? Look who's talking.'' He laughed at that, and she found herself laughing with him.

They ate a leisurely meal and then lingered a while, talking easily about day-to-day things. He told her his ideas for improving Daniel's small herd of Black Angus. And she joked about how Jerry over at the *Clarion* had finally broken down and bought some new equipment. Now they could do almost everything on computer.

"Jerry offered me a full-time job last week,'' she told him. "Not that he hasn't done that every summer for the past three years.''

"Thinking of changing your plans?'' Did he look hopeful—that she might change her mind and decide to stay in town? Or simply curious? She really couldn't tell.

She shook her head. "The day after Labor Day I'm off to the big city to make my mark. I've been planning it for a long time and I'm not turning back now.''

His expression was...what? Kind of admiring, maybe? He nodded. "That's good. Hold on to that dream until you make it real.''

His hand rested on the table. She couldn't resist laying hers over it. "I will,'' she promised low.

He turned his hand over and clasped hers. For a long, delicious moment, they just sat there, holding hands across the table. She reveled in the feel of his rough, warm palm against hers, in the excitement that seemed to charge the air between them.

She found she was looking at his mouth, recalling those secret long-ago kisses they'd stolen the few times they'd managed to sneak away behind the hay bales in the barn, or in the shadows of the tack room— or once, out in the trees by Crystal Creek, which ran along behind the homesteader's cabin way out back behind the barn.

A slow heat was moving through her. So incredible to be here, with him, like this. She never would have believed it could happen.

And she couldn't help thinking, *I'm all grown up now. We won't have to sneak around anymore....*

It was barely dark when they got up to go. Way too early to call it a night as far as Starr was concerned. "We could stop in at Mustang Sally's for a little while," she suggested.

"Sure. If you'd like that."

Mustang Sally's, about five miles out of town on the way to Sheridan, was a bar with a dance floor and pool tables, and rooms in back where the card players gathered. The jukebox was always cranked up too loud. A blue haze of cigarette smoke fogged the air, mingling with the yeasty, sour smell of stale beer.

It was not the Four Seasons, but Starr didn't care. She was with Beau.

They ordered a couple of longnecks and claimed a corner booth and got up to dance whenever some kind soul bucked the trend and played a slow song. The rest of the time they sat in the shadows and whispered together.

After the third slow, lovely dance, they returned to the table with their arms around each other. When they slid into the booth, he pulled her right up against him.

It was just the most natural, right and perfect thing, to lean even closer, to tip her mouth up....

His mouth descended. Those eyes, blue as the summer sky, rayed in white around the iris if you looked real close, drifted shut. His lips brushed hers—back and forth, as if seeking the right fit.

"Oh, Beau," she whispered, and pulled on his collar, urging him to deepen the kiss.

He didn't need a lot of encouragement. His mouth closed over hers and she turned into him, pressing close, sliding her arms up his hard chest to link around his neck.

The kiss went on and on. It seemed like it would never end and that was just fine with her. The smoky room, the loud, jangling country song on the jukebox, the crows of triumph from some guy across the room at the old-time pinball machine—all of it receded.

There was nothing but Beau's mouth on hers, his breath across her cheek, his arms holding her so close and warm, his hands rubbing her back...

He was the one to stop it, before they started tearing each other's clothes off right there in the booth. "We'd better go..." His voice was husky with a thrilling combination of need and regret.

"Yeah," she whispered, breathless. Yearning. "Yeah, I guess so."

* * *

Starr sat tucked against Beau's side as they drove through the night. He had the radio turned to a retro-rock station. Groups that had been around when her father was a little kid played the classics from the sixties and seventies, the sounds jangling and yet somehow comforting at the same time.

Neither of them said much. He had his right arm tight around her—though they both knew very well he should have had both hands on the wheel. Once or twice he turned his head to breathe a kiss into her hair.

She leaned all the closer, kissing his neck, rubbing her head against his shirt, even turning her mouth to his chest once or twice, planting a kiss there, through the warm fabric of his shirt. She could hear his heart beating, strong and steady and little bit urgent, against her ear.

She breathed in the smell of him, a fresh, green smell, like clove—and something else, too. Something earthy and all about his being a man.

She shouldn't have maybe, but she couldn't resist running a hand over his chest, down to his belt and around to clasp the hard-muscled side of his waist. The temptation was great to be really bad, to let her hand stray lower. But he *was* trying to drive. She was making him crazy enough as it was. His breathing—and hers too—went past urgent and on through to down-right ragged.

They'd left the highway and were bumping along on a side road, drift fences and the shadows of cattle out in the pastures on either side rolling by, when Beau swung the wheel sharply to the right. They turned down another road, a narrower one, and rolled under the deep shadow of a cottonwood tree. He switched off the engine and the song on the radio ended in midnote.

That left the pounding of their two hearts, the sound of the urgent, heavy breathing they were both trying to control—and out the open window, the whisper of the ever-present wind, the sweet cries of night birds....

And something else. Another whispering, rushing sound.

She looked up, tipping her head way back, seeking his eyes from the cradle of his arms. "Crystal Creek?"

His lips touched her forehead, hot with promise. "Yeah." He put a finger under her chin to lift her mouth up.

And then he kissed her—a deep, claiming kiss. His mouth sucked at hers, drawing her tongue out, taking it in. He swept his tongue around it, the rough-slippery surface sliding up, over and down...

She moaned in delight as he shifted her in his arms, till she lay across him, supported by his cradling arm against the door, the steering wheel containing them, tight to each other.

He went on kissing her. She heard the trilling of crickets, the soft cries of the birds—and her own breath, coming hard and uneven, catching now and then on a hungry sigh.

She said his name, "Beau..." and she gasped in wonder as his hand found her breast, molding it, claiming it. He lifted his head to look down at her. She moaned and his fingers were quick, undoing the little buttons down the front of her lace-trimmed shirt.

He peeled the two sides of the shirt away, laying it open to reveal her breasts, pale as milk in the starlight, swelling from her satin bra. He cradled one, then pressed his palm flat against the nipple. It drew up inside the cup of her bra, so hard and tight and aching. She arched her back and cried his name once more.

His mouth found hers again, demanding and hot, as his hand strayed around to her back. She turned into him with a moan, losing the hungry hold of his lips, giving him easier access to the clasp of her bra. It gave in an instant and the bra fell loose.

She sighed. "Oh," she whispered, "oh, yes…"

With a hungry cry, she lifted her mouth to his. They kissed some more, long and deep and wet, as he guided the bra and the shirt off one arm. He urged her up. She let go of his mouth yet another time, long enough to get clear of the steering wheel and struggle out of the shirt, to peel the bra down her other arm and toss them both to the floorboards.

"So beautiful," he whispered, "Always so beautiful—so beautiful it hurts…" She lay back in his arms and he bent his golden head.

He took her breast in his mouth, softly circling her nipple with his tongue, then catching it lightly between his teeth, holding it there, worrying it, his tongue flicking and licking…

She clutched his head and cried out and his hand strayed along the bare skin over her rib cage, moving around to the front of her, pausing at her navel, searching…

He found the tiny platinum ring she wore there and gave it a tug. She moaned and felt him smile against her breast before he again sucked her nipple in and toyed with it some more.

His rough-tender fingers danced lower, unsnapping

the front of her jeans, guiding the zipper down. It made a low, sizzling sound as it parted. She cradled his silky head, pulled him tighter into her, urging him to suck all the harder....

Below, his fingers slipped in, under her satin panties. He swallowed her cries of need as he petted the nest of curls down there...

Gently, insistently, he guided her legs a little apart, so he could dip a finger between the slick folds.

She was on fire by then, writhing against him, clutching his shoulders, wanting his lips on hers. He raised his mouth from her breast and he kissed her— a deep, never-ending kiss....

His finger dipped lower still, easing inside of her, his knuckles hindered a little by the rough cover of her tight jeans. She moaned into his mouth and felt her own body clutch around him, felt the shocking liquid slide as he moved his finger in and out.

"Tight," he muttered against her mouth. "So tight, so wet..."

Should she have stopped him, or at least slowed things up a little? Should they have talked, so he'd know?

Yeah, she should have.

But what she should have done meant nothing. Not right then. Right then, her mind was a frantic fog of starved yearning. And in her deepest heart, in the place where she was all woman, she had always known. Always. That it would be Beau. Even when she'd thought she hated him, she'd known he would be the one.

She whispered, "You, Beau...only you..."

And after that, it got fast and furious and frantic—

and awkward, too, as he took her shoulders, guided her around, pushed her back to the passenger side, shifting himself so he could grab her jeans and her panties, slithering them down. They were boot-cut jeans, but still they got snagged on her impractical kitten-heeled boots, so he levered back fast and unzipped the boots, yanking them off, one and then the other. They dropped with twin knocking sounds against the floor. He tossed her jeans and panties down there after them.

He ripped off his own shirt, threw it down, undid his Wranglers, shoved them out of the way. That brought her up short—when she saw him. He was so big and thick, kind of silky-looking, standing out straight from a shadowy nest of hair. She blinked—but she wasn't giving up on this.

Oh, no. She had been waiting. Waiting so long…

In her mind was that long-ago afternoon in the barn before Tess interrupted them and everything went wrong. She could almost hear the far-off whinny of one of the horses out in the pasture in back, could faintly smell the ripe scent of the hay bale they leaned against, sharpened with the dryness of dust. Her body thrummed with the thrill of his body so close, so hungry for her….

It was the same now: the urgency. The feeling of rightness. The delicious thrill of apprehension for what would come next.

She lay back along the seat, her head bumping the armrest.

She shut her eyes….

And steeled herself for the pain.

But it didn't come. He had paused, there, between

her open legs. She dared to stop squeezing her eyes shut and peeked up at him.

He was so fine to look at, silvered in the starlight that filled the cab. She relaxed a little, just at the purely male sight of him, his chest broad and strong, dusted with the same gold hair that grew below his washboard belly, his arms corded with muscle, and his face…oh, he looked at her as if she was the only woman on earth.

Mine, she thought. *Always. Mine….*

Scars marred the golden perfection of his skin— white puckering ones. Some were slice-marks, thin and ridged, some were round—those ranged in size, some very small, some as big as a nickel. She'd seen the scars before, but in daylight all those years ago, when she'd caught him with his shirt off. He'd been hauling bags of feed into the barn. She'd lured him deeper into the shadows where no one would see them.

And she'd asked him why his chest and back were scarred up so bad.

She could still recall his answer. "From things that cut—and from things that burn."

"But who would do that?"

He'd given a low, mean-sounding laugh. "You musta never met my daddy. And don't worry, you never will. He's been dead for a while. But then, there's still my brothers, T.J. and Lyle…"

Lyle was dead too, now. Stabbed in a prison-yard scuffle four years ago. T.J. was still living—at the moment. He had his own private cell on death row down at Rawlins. He'd been out of prison a week—after serving his time for rustling Rising Sun cattle—when he shot a police officer during the commission of a gas-station robbery.

Now, in the starlight, the cruel marks on Beau's body had a strange, pale kind of beauty. In their whiteness, they almost seemed to glow. She reached up, traced a long, thin one that ran from his shoulder almost to his elbow.

Before she reached the base of that scar, he moved his arm away, out from under her touch, and sat back on his folded-under legs, wide shoulders slumping. "It shouldn't be like this," he whispered, his voice rough with conflicting emotions: deepest regret—burning desire. "In this old pickup..."

At first, she felt embarrassment, lying there all spread out and naked except for a pair of thin socks. She pulled her knees together and crossed her arms over her bare breasts. But then her heart kind of...opened, at the pure hunger and yearning, the real need in his eyes. She felt that same need....

With a cry, she reached up, beckoning.

He levered himself over her, still up on his knees, but close enough now that she could stroke his cheek. He moved his head, his mouth sliding into the cove of her palm, pressing a kiss there. "You want to stop? Say so..."

But she didn't say anything. Somehow, she couldn't. She could only look up at him and wish for his mouth to settle on hers again. She could only long for what was so close, for the feel of his hot, strong body pressing her down.

She had some vague idea that they wouldn't quite make love all the way, that she'd gently whisper her secret before it got to that. Even then, somewhere in some logical corner of her mind, she knew she was telling herself one whopping lie. She was all but naked, one bare thigh to either side of his lean hips. There was nothing, not one single layer of fabric between the cove of her sex and his ready manhood. Nothing but the darkness, the mild summer-night air.

She knew they weren't going to stop—but she told herself that somehow they would, anyway.

He began to stroke her body, one hand on each thigh, his palms trailing up, over the sides of her waist, along the curves over her rib cage, to the sides of her breasts and back down again. He caressed her belly, both hands moving in and then brushing back down again to the tops of her thighs. He bent his golden head and lightly nipped her navel ring, taking it between his teeth for one sharp little tug.

She squirmed and called his name some more, her voice strange, low and guttural, to her own ears. His mouth brushed, soft as velvet, over and down. He stuck out his tongue and traced the tiny ladybug in the hollow of her hipbone. "Here it is," he whispered against her burning flesh, "that secret tattoo…"

The one only the right man is gonna see, she was thinking. Thinking it like a promise. A promise to *him…*

He slid his hands upward, so his thumbs touched her, parted her…

And then his mouth was there, covering her most private place. She moaned and tossed her head and put her hands up and back, palms flat, to press the door, lifting her hips to him, giving him greater access.

Oh, that, oh yes… His mouth covering her—that was heaven. A little bit of heaven right there in the cab of an old green pickup truck. His tongue dipped in and then slid along all the soft, wet surfaces. He found the little nub where her pleasure was greatest. And...

Oh, she had never...

Never even imagined.

It was...

She was...

Opening, her whole body quivering in a quicksilver rushing sensation, one that started as a faint, shivering glow and grew brighter, more powerful, shimmering its way all through her, moving outward, growing brighter. Stronger. Bigger.

She moaned and she cried out as a hot, joyous pulsing began.

And right then, when the whole world seemed to fly away, when she tossed her head and moaned so deep and pushed against the door to help her press herself closer to his pleasuring mouth...

Right then...

He slid up her body and entered her in one hard, tearing thrust.

Chapter Five

They cried out together—she at the sudden, searing pain, he in pure shock. He stared down into her face and she let out a second cry. He looked...so hurt. Hurt much worse than she was, injured some deep and awful way.

"Starr..." He said her name as if she had done something terrible to him, as if she'd pulled out a knife and stabbed him to the heart.

She couldn't bear it, the wounded accusation in his eyes. She reached for him, pulling his mouth down to hers.

He resisted, his upper body tight, scorning her clutching hands, even while his hips stayed pressing into her—as if the part of him that was most male couldn't bear to leave her.

"Beau," she whispered. "Beau, please..."

She felt him quiver and a strange hot surge of triumph shot through her, at her power over him. He couldn't hold out against her....

With a long, shuddering sigh, he gave in. His mouth covered hers and he kissed her, a plundering, hungry kind of kiss. And down there, deep inside, where he stretched her tender body beyond its virgin limits, he was pulsing, kind of twitching. Through the burning pain, she felt him spilling into her as he pressed so tight against her, as if, since that first painful thrust, he didn't dare to move.

With a low, lost groan, he went lax and heavy on top of her—but only for a second or two. Then he levered back. She let out another cry at the pain of him pulling free. He reached for the glove box, snapped it open and yanked out a small box of tissues.

He swiftly wiped himself dry and rose fully to his knees to pull up his Wranglers and fasten them. Then he turned his attention to her. She felt...really bad then. Really bad and really naked. He'd backed toward the driver's side enough that she could draw her legs together. She tried that. He caught her right knee before it could meet the left.

He swore. "You're bleeding..."

"Listen," she said between clenched teeth—and then had no idea what to say next. So she crossed her arms over her breasts and scooted back enough that she could swing her stocking feet to the floorboards. She bent and started snatching up her clothes.

"Starr..." The tenderness in his voice made her pause, clutching her shirt and her bra, bent over to cover as much as she could. "Starr." He touched her back—a tentative caress, questioning as his worried tone.

She dropped the clothes and put her hands over her face. A dry sob welled up. She tried to cut it off, but it shook her body anyway.

"Starr." He clasped her bare shoulder in a steadying kind of way, his hand so warm and reassuringly firm. "Damn my soul to hell, I am so sorry…" She pressed her hands to her burning cheeks, sucked in one long breath and let it out with slow care as he slid over right next to her. "Come on. Come here…" He took both her shoulders and gathered her into him.

With another dry sob, she surrendered to his embrace, cuddling in close, burying her face in the dusting of springy hair on his broad chest.

He stroked her hair, rubbed her back. "It's okay," he said. "It'll be okay…" He rubbed his chin against her hair, whispered, "I swear to you. I would have stopped, if I had known, if you had only said something…"

She turned her mouth to his shoulder, brushed a kiss against one of the white welts of scar tissue and breathed her confession against that scar. "I know you would have…"

He put a finger under her chin, coaxing her head up and asked, in a whisper both tender and slightly bewildered, "Then damn it, why didn't you tell me?"

She smiled at that, a quivery smile, and she thought of what women always say at times like that one. "If you don't know, I'm sure not going to tell you…."

He was shaking his head. "I just don't get it."

She put a hand against his warm chest, felt his heart

beating under her palm. "Oh, I think you do. Somewhere in here, I think you really do."

He frowned. But he didn't argue—or admit that he understood. He only asked, sky-blue eyes darkened with concern, "Does it…still hurt?"

She scrunched up her nose at him. "Yeah. It stings.…"

He bent his head for a last, quick kiss. "Come on, then." He hauled a blanket from behind the seat. "Let's go on down to the creek for a few minutes.…"

He gathered her clothes and his shirt off the floorboards, shook them out and laid them over the back of the seat as she put on her boots and wrapped the blanket, sarong-style, around her. The blood—only a little bit, really—had dried to tackiness between her thighs. She tried to be careful not to get it on the blanket, though the dark plaid probably wouldn't show the stain.

"Ready?" he asked, as she tucked the blanket in place. She nodded. He got out and came around and opened her door for her, putting out a hand to guide her down. His arm firm and steadying around her shoulders, he led her out from under the shadowing branches of the tree.

The night was so beautiful, clear and cool, the stars sparkling like a million tiny crystal beads twinkling on a black velvet gown.

She stopped, entranced, staring up at that glorious sky. "Oh, Beau. What a night, huh?"

He made a grudging noise of agreement, his mind obviously on moving along. "Come on."

The little pointy heels on her boots were not made

for walking in the dirt. She tried to tread carefully, but still she stumbled.

"Silly boots," he muttered.

She poked him with an elbow. "I love these boots."

"Here." He scooped her up against his warm, hard chest.

"Well," she said, twining her hands around his neck. "This is nice…" She laid her head against his shoulder and thought about the lie she'd told herself the week before—the one about how she wouldn't be jumping his bones.

That made her giggle.

"Stop squirming," he commanded, so she swallowed that giggle down—but allowed herself a smug little smile, nonetheless.

It wasn't far, back under the shadowing trees. The creek wound past, shimmering in starlight, catching the waning shape of the moon, reflecting it back at them, a shape that wavered with the current. He eased her to her feet and she sat on the bank to take off her boots and her socks. Once her feet were bare, he helped her up again and led her down to the water's edge.

She shivered when she waded into it, wrapping her arms around herself. "Brr…"

"Better let me take the blanket."

There were trees on either side of the bank, sheltering them from sight should someone drive by out on the narrow dirt road, or even come riding through the pasture beyond the fence on the far side. She sent him a sideways glance. "Promise you won't look."

"You have my sworn word."

He said it so seriously, she couldn't help laughing.

"Oh, Beau. I was just teasing—I mean, it's not like you haven't pretty much seen all there is to see." She giggled some more and shivered as the icy water lapped at her ankles.

He was looking worried again. "I'd better help you." He dropped to the bank and yanked off his boots and socks and then came in with her.

She shivered some more. "Your jeans are getting wet."

"Don't worry about that—here." He went behind her and she turned her head to watch what he was up to. "Give me the blanket…"

She held on to it tighter. "Only if you'll get that look off your face."

He scowled. "What look?"

"That one." She pointed at him over her shoulder. "Really serious. Downright grim."

He forced a silly fake smile. "Better?"

"Not much."

"The blanket. Come on."

"Oh, all right." She untucked the blanket and handed him the ends. He opened it wide, raising it so it wouldn't touch the water. She shivered all the harder as the night air touched all of her—well, except for her feet, which were still in the water and felt halfway numb by then.

"Just a few steps," he said softly, coaxingly. "In the center, it'll be deep enough you can rinse off."

So she felt her way over the sharp rocks to the middle of the narrow stream, where she dipped down and rinsed herself. The icy water put goose bumps on her goose bumps, but where it mattered, it did feel good. She sighed in pleasure as the stinging eased and the smears of blood were rinsed away. Too bad her teeth were chattering…

"Better?" he asked.

"Yeah." She stood. "But now I am *freezing*."

"Let's go then…" He kind of herded her back to the bank, where he wrapped the blanket around her again and tucked it in place—but not tight enough. It started to slip off the moment he let go of it.

She caught it. "Here. Let me…" Tucking it properly, she turned in his arms and rested her hands against his chest, seeking his eyes through the darkness. "Beau. Please try to understand." He made a grumbling sound. She went on anyway. "I…I wanted it to be you. I always did, I think since the day I first saw you, that first day I came back to the Rising Sun to live. You rode into the yard at the house in the bed of one of Dad's pickups. You stood up when you saw me, remember? You stood up and took off your hat and put it over your heart. I remember my dad said, 'Get your tongue back in your mouth, Tisdale.' Remember that?" He made a grumbly sound. She added, "You had me, that first time we saw each other. You know you did."

He gave her a look. She would always remember it, that look—treasure it, safe in her heart where she kept all the very best memories. It was a look both tender and full of wonderment. "I think you are a little bit crazy, Starr." The words were husky—and full of the same wonderment she saw in his face.

"Yeah," she whispered back. "I think I am. But trust me. It's a good kind of crazy." She slid her hands up to link behind his neck. "And now we're lovers, aren't we?'' It came out as a challenge—which was exactly what she'd meant it to be.

He narrowed his eyes at her. He had his hands at her waist, and he pushed her away a little—to a safer distance, maybe. ''Where are you leading with this?''

''I'm cold and I want you to wrap your arms around me. Please?''

He muttered a swear word, but he did it.

Her shivers subsided, eased in an instant by his body's warmth. She nuzzled his neck, breathed in the scent of him. ''Umm. Much better.'' She kissed his chin. ''I just want you to know that this was…what I wanted.''

He grunted. ''Yeah. In an old pickup truck—and way too rough for an innocent woman. Real romantic.''

She kind of shoved at him with a shoulder. ''Stop that. It *was* romantic. And I'm not innocent, not in my heart. I never was. Not when it came to you.'' He was scowling again. She reached up and traced his brows, soothing that scowl away. ''Beau Tisdale, don't you know? It's not where, or even how. It's *who*. It's two people together, in an honest, open way. Both of them saying *yes*, you know? Each really wanting to be with the other. That's what matters when it comes to something like this.''

He grumbled, ''You still should have told me.''

''Yeah. I should have. But I didn't. It happened the way it happened. And it's…okay with me.'' She snuggled in closer with a happy sigh. ''It was with you, Beau. Just like I always knew it would be.''

His arms tightened around her. ''Now what?''

She lifted her head from the hollow of his shoulder

and met his eyes. "Well, now we have this summer, for us. We can be together. *Really* together like we couldn't be all those years ago." She threaded her fingers up into the silky hair at his nape. "So I think you should kiss me now. Don't you?"

His eyes gleamed down at her. The crickets sang and the creek burbled by at their feet and she knew she was exactly where she wanted to be. Held close in Beau's arms under the summer stars.

At last, he asked roughly, "That's all you want, a kiss?"

"No. I told you. I want *you*. For the summer. But for right now, say yes. And then kiss me. That would be so nice."

"Nice," he repeated, irritatingly doubtful.

"Yeah, nice. Say yes. Please."

He looked at her for a long time. And then, at last, he whispered, "Yes."

And then he kissed her, long and deep.

Chapter Six

After that night, they spent every spare second together, though it was never as much time as they wished it could be. Beau, after all, had a ranch to run. Starr had her job at the paper, plus Tess and Edna expected her to do her bit around the house. So she washed dishes and ran the vacuum and weeded Tess's garden and peeled any vegetable that was set in front of her—and waited for the next time she could be with Beau.

They went to the Wednesday-night rodeo at the county fairgrounds and on Friday, Starr cooked dinner for Daniel and Beau. Saturday, they drove up to Sheridan to see a movie....

And they made each other crazy in the cab of that green pickup, parking under the cottonwoods down by the creek, acting like a couple of sex-obsessed teenagers and reveling in every caress, every hungry, wet kiss. Those first few times they were alone together after the night she so shocked him by giving him her virginity, Beau refused to go beyond starved kisses and urgent caresses. He didn't want to hurt her.

She was okay with that—at first, anyway. She *was* a little sore. So they would kiss and stroke each other until Starr felt certain her body was going to incinerate with the heat between them. And then, panting and unsatisfied, they'd pull apart. They'd talk for a while, there in the cab, or walk down by the creek until they both had a chance to cool off a little. Then he would drive her home.

After Saturday night, Starr was getting pretty tired of lovemaking that stopped short of all the way. This was *their* summer, after all. They weren't going to be spending every tender moment in the cab of an old truck. No way.

They deserved a bed—but not just any old bed.

Though they weren't hiding anything, neither of them wanted to flaunt what they shared. Beau lived in the house with Daniel now. The sweet old guy didn't need a couple of lovers having wild sex in one of his bedrooms. And Starr's room—upstairs at the Rising Sun, with her dad and Tess across the hall and Jobeth a wall away? Uh-uh. That was not going to be happening.

They could find some motel, she supposed.

But no. That *would* be like sneaking around. And they weren't lovers like that. They were *discreet*. She smiled as she thought the word. Yeah. *Discreet.* They might try a motel room, one time, for a thrill. But they deserved a place to be together, a private space they could claim as their own.

And really, now she thought about it, wasn't it about time she had her own private space at the Rising Sun? Edna had the foreman's cottage, across the yard in front, so that was out. There were trailers, for the hands. One of them was vacant now.

But no, she didn't think she wanted to take over one of the trailers....

That left the old homesteader's cabin, past the barn and beyond the horse pasture, not far from where the creek ran by. Four years ago, her dad had put in electricity out there. It had running water and it was fully furnished—in a rustic kind of way, with old mismatched pieces that had been handed down in the family for generations.

Rustic, Starr decided, was fine with her. She had a distant cousin, an artist named Lacey, who'd come from California few years ago and stayed in the cabin for a while. Lacey had been pregnant when she arrived, seven months or so. At nine months along, her baby's father, Logan, had come to find her.

Logan ended up delivering their baby—right there, in the cabin. They got married in the great room of the main house and then they went home to California.

Starr had thought it all terribly romantic. Logan was a dark-haired hunk of a guy. And Starr admired Lacey—her free, adventurous spirit and her open smile. Lacey had loved living in the cabin....

At breakfast that Sunday morning, Starr told the family—and the hands, since they were there—what she planned. "I'd like to move into the homesteader's cabin for the summer," she said. "I think I'll make the move today.'' She gave them all a big smile. ''Is that okay?''

''But why?'' Edna asked. ''You'll be much more comfortable here in the main house. And what about that fancy computer of yours? You won't be able to get the Internet out there.''

''I can use my room upstairs for an office, do my work there.'' Starr speared up a bite of scrambled eggs. ''And as far as being comfortable, I think I'll like it in the cabin.''

''But—'' That was as far as Edna got, because Zach cut her off.

''The cabin's yours if you want it,'' her dad said so easily, she wanted to leap up and run down the table and throw her arms around him. ''Tim, can you turn the water on out there this morning?''

''Sure can, Zach.''

''And maybe you can give Starr a hand with whatever she needs moved.''

The old cowboy beamed, the wrinkles etching all the deeper in his leathery face. ''Glad to be of help.''

Edna sighed. ''Well, well. I think I will eat my breakfast and mind my own business now.'' Nobody argued with her.

The one-room cabin was musty-smelling after so long without an occupant.

Starr braced open the front and rear doors to air things out. She shook out the cover on the daybed that served as a sofa, made up the double bed in the curtained-off nook in the corner. She put her clothes away in the old bureau and set out a few personal treasures she'd brought over from the main house. After Tim had the water running, she washed up the dusty dishes. And she wiped down all the counters and shelves. Then she sat at the round pine table and made herself a grocery list.

By noon she was ready to head for town to buy what she needed. She stopped in at the main house on the way out and called Beau. He was there, as she'd expected, sharing the mid-day meal with Daniel.

"Come to dinner at my house. Tonight. Six o'clock," she said. And then she told him that her house was the homesteader's cabin now. "I moved in today."

"Why?" he said.

"You sound just like Edna—and take a wild guess."

She heard his breath catch as he figured it out. "Dinner, huh?" His voice was low now, soft as velvet.

"Yeah. Six. Don't be late."

When she got back from town, she put the groceries away and then went down to the creek to pick a bouquet of wildflowers. She put them in a Mason jar on the table and stood back to admire them.

Her own place. With her own bouquet of flowers on the table. Yeah, she'd had apartments before, in Boulder, during her junior and senior years at C.U. But this was different. This was her own place…at home. And that was something pretty special, something she hadn't even realized she wanted until now.

Someone knocked at the rough plank door. Her first guest in her own place. She called out a cheery "Come on in."

The door swung inward. It was Tess. One look at her stepmother's face told Starr everything.

"Got a minute or two?"

Starr supposed she'd known this was coming. "A little talk, right? Just between us…"

Tess nodded. "That's right. Just us."

Starr indicated a chair. "I have lemonade."

"Yes. Please."

Starr poured out two glasses and sat in the straight-back chair opposite Tess. They each took a sip, more or less in unison, and then set their glasses down.

"Pretty flowers," said Tess.

Starr adjusted a wild iris in her makeshift vase. "It's about Beau and me, right?" Tess nodded. Her lips were kind of pressed together. Starr asked, "Did Dad send you over here?"

The corners of Tess's mouth turned up then, a smile as sweet as it was wistful. "Oh, honey. Haven't you realized by now that your dad thinks that Beau's the perfect man for you?"

Starr blinked. She had a kind of hollow feeling in her stomach. And then that feeling turned to a fluttery warmth. "Uh…he does?"

Tess sipped her lemonade. "It's not all that surprising, really, if you think about it. You know how your dad is. He admires nothing so much as a hard-working, honest man."

In her mind's eye, Starr saw Beau's face—the firm jaw, the direct way he would look at her. "He is, isn't he? A good, honest man."

"That he is. In the years since all that trouble— with you, and with his brothers—Beau has proved over and over that he's just the kind of man your father respects and admires.'' A gleam lit Tess's dark eyes. ''And the fact that Daniel's made Beau his heir doesn't hurt, either, though it's truly not the determining factor.''

Starr sat back a little. ''You know about Daniel's will? Beau had me promise not to tell anyone.''

''Daniel told your father, back when he made the decision, a couple of years ago—and I mean it. It's not the main reason your dad thinks you and Beau are a match.''

''A match.'' Starr was getting the picture. She wasn't very comfortable with it. ''You're saying…as in marriage?''

''Yes. As in marriage.''

Their glasses were sweating. Starr got up, went to the counter, and tore a couple of paper towels off the roll. She handed one to Tess. They folded them into squares and slid them beneath their glasses. Then there was one of those moments: two women—mother and daughter at heart; friends as well—regarding each other steadily across a table.

Star broke the silence. ''Beau and I aren't talking about marriage. His life is here….''

''That's right. And you have a few plans for yourself.''

Starr fiddled with the edge of her makeshift coaster. ''Well, what are you saying? Are you trying to talk me into breaking it off with him?''

Tess put her hand on her stomach, which looked pretty flat to Starr, though she was well into her third month of pregnancy. ''No. It's not my place to do such a thing.''

"So…Dad, then? He's expecting that we'll end up married?"

Tess got that wistful smile again. "I'm only saying he would approve and be glad if you did. But your father's a smart man. He knows better than to try and plan out other people's lives for them—even if one of those people is his own precious daughter." Tess gave her a sideways look. "Now, Edna. She's another story…"

Starr almost rolled her eyes. "Tell me about it."

Tess's gaze was straight-on now. "Edna's protective—of you and of your own dreams for yourself. But even Edna knows that two adults will do what they want to do with their lives, in the end."

"So…?"

Tess shifted in the hard chair. "Oh, I guess it's only…well, you've felt so strongly for Beau for such a long time now—adoring him or hating him, he's never been all that far from your mind. Has he?"

Starr thought about that, thought about the boys she'd dated in high school, the guys she'd known in college. All of them she remembered in shades of gray. Not Beau. Thoughts of Beau were bold and shining, in living color. "Yeah," she admitted. "Beau is…special to me. But we both know, Beau and me, that we want different things from life. All we're asking for is one summer together. Is that such a bad thing?"

"No. Of course not. It's not a bad thing at all. I suppose I only wanted to be sure you've thought this through, that you're not getting involved in something that will steal your dreams away—or leave you with your heart in pieces. Or maybe a little bit of both."

Starr realized she was biting the inside of her lip. "That's what you think will happen? That I'll give up my plans for myself, or end up with my heart broken? Does every relationship between a man and a woman that doesn't end in marriage have to break hearts or shatter somebody's dreams?"

"That depends on the man…and the woman, I guess."

Starr put her elbows on the table and leaned toward her stepmother. "I'm not giving him up, Tess."

"Listen to yourself." Tess's eyes were so soft. "Hear the passion in your own voice. Do you honestly think you're going to be able to walk away from that man without it ripping you apart inside when the summer's over?"

"The summer's barely started…."

"Think again. August is just about here. Five weeks, and it's over, you're off for New York—and let's not fight. I truly didn't come here for that."

Starr slumped back in her chair. "Coulda fooled me."

Tess only shrugged. "I just think, sometimes, when you want something so badly, it's tempting to tell yourself lies about what you're doing, that's all. Tempting to say, 'Oh, it's only for the summer,' as if a summer wasn't long enough to end in a broken heart."

Starr picked up her glass—and plunked it down without drinking from it. "I just don't get where you're headed with this."

Tess frowned—and then she sighed. "Don't…fool yourself. That's all I want to say, I think. Lies are no good, especially the kind of lies you tell to yourself."

"You think I'm lying to myself?"

"I think maybe you care for Beau a whole lot more than you're letting yourself admit—and you know, the more I listen to myself talk, the more fed up I become with myself."

Starr's irritation faded. She found she could laugh. "Well, I'm going to take your advice to heart—as soon as I can figure out what it is you're saying."

Tess leaned closer. "You know, I think what I'm really telling you is, I'm here. I'm your stepmother, yes. But I truly am also your friend. It may sound as if I'm telling you what to do, but really, I'm just worrying out loud. Yes, your dad thinks this romance between you and Beau is the best thing that could have happened to either of you. I'm a little more cautious. I can't see how it could work out, unless one of you ends up living where you don't want to be. But whatever happens, your dad and I are with you. We'll support you in whatever you decide is right for your life."

After Tess left, Starr took a while choosing the clothes she would wear that night. Once she'd decided, she laid the clothes on the bed and took clean jeans and a T-shirt out to the bathroom, a makeshift affair housed in a lean-to off the back of the cabin. She had a nice, long soak in the old clawfoot tub out there and tried not to think of some of the things Tess had said— the part about lying to herself, about how she cared more for Beau than she was admitting...

Well, maybe she did. Maybe she was going to end up with her heart ripped in two at the end of the summer.

So be it. She'd meant what she said to Tess: she wasn't giving their summer up. No way.

And *five weeks?* Was it really only five weeks until the summer ended? Mentally, she counted the days and discovered that Tess had it right.

Dang it. You'd think Tess might have just kept that little bit of information to herself....

So you can lie to yourself?

"Oh, shut up," she said to that self-righteous, prissy little voice in her head. She ducked under the water to get away from it, and when she came back up, she turned up the boom box she'd set on the wicker stand by the tub. She sang along to a favorite CD—loudly— to keep herself from thinking any more depressing thoughts.

Back in the cabin, she did battle with the old wood-stove, got the fire laid and lit. Once the temperature had more or less stabilized, she stuck a chicken in there to roast, opening all three of the windows to keep the place from overheating. She had carrots and new potatoes. Those, she wrapped in foil with butter and spices. They'd go in a little later....

When the green pickup appeared, right on time, rolling toward her from the road that led around the horse pasture, she was sitting on the front step waiting for him in the clothes she'd chosen earlier. She had a sort of rising feeling, a kind of lightness that made her want to lift right up off that step and float on out to meet him.

She let the thrill shimmer through her and she stayed right there on the step. He pulled to a stop in the clear space next to her Suburban. She stayed right where she was, grinning like a long-gone fool, as he got out and came around the front of pickup. He strode toward her on those long, muscular legs and her stomach hollowed out, then flooded with a lovely warmth. He stopped right in front of her, one hand held suspiciously behind his back.

"Welcome to my new home." She braced her chin on the heel of her hand and went on grinning.

He sniffed the air. "Something cookin' in there?" His eyes spoke of intimate things.

The warmth in her belly went more or less molten. "Oh, yeah—and what are you hiding?"

"Nothin' much." He held out a bouquet of black-eyed Susans. The cheery yellow flowers with their velvet-brown centers grew wild in open pastures and along the roadsides. He must have stopped to pick them for her....

"Oh, Beau." She took them, rising. "They're beautiful." She reached for his hand. "Come on." She tugged him up the two steps, across the slightly rickety porch and in the door, where she gestured at the table. "Sit down."

He pulled out a chair and watched as she got another jar, filled it with water, and set it on the counter by the sink. She put the flowers in it, taking a moment or two to pull at the stems, so none of the golden daisylike petals were bent. Once she had them arranged to her liking, she put them at the place of honor on the table and moved the others to the top of the bureau.

He caught her hand as she went past his chair. One little tug, and she was sitting in his lap, her full black skirt, printed with red cherries, falling all the way to the rough planks of the floor.

He put his hand on her knee. "Nice skirt."

"Why, thank you." It was fifties-style, what they used to call a circle skirt. On top, she wore a black camisole with a built-in bra and a sheer lawn shirt, also black. She was going for a sort of hostessy look—but sexy, too.

The light in his eyes said she'd hit the mark on the sexy part, at least. He took a handful of the skirt in his tanned fist and started pulling, gathering it up, peeling back all those cherries to reveal her bare legs, inch by slow inch.

Her breath caught. He only smiled and kept on sliding the skirt up and up. And up some more...

When he got it past her knees, she caught his wrist. "I should probably check my chicken...."

He nuzzled her neck. "I'll check your chicken for you."

She punched his shoulder. "Oh, I'll bet you will..." His mouth was right there, not an inch from hers. She whispered, "That chicken can wait..."

"You sure?"

She nodded. Slowly. "Kiss me."

He didn't argue, just covered her lips with his own.

Chapter Seven

With a long, shuddering sigh, Starr wrapped both arms around Beau's neck and gave him her mouth. That knowing hand of his stroked her thigh, pushing her skirt back, moving higher, inch by slow inch, leaving pleasured goose bumps in its wake.

A husky giggle rising in her throat, she slid off his lap. He made a protesting sound against her lips. But then he sighed when she only sat right back down, facing him this time, one leg to either side of his hips, her big skirt falling around them, covering the place where her black lace panties pressed against the bulging front of his jeans.

Shamelessly, she rocked back and forth on that bulge. His kiss deepened even more, his tongue sweeping her mouth. He moaned as he clutched her bottom in both hands and yanked her up all the tighter against him.

Then his lips slid down, over her chin, along her neck. He nipped little kisses against her throat and she stretched it back for him, moaning his name.

Right there at the table, he unbuttoned her see-through shirt and pushed it over her shoulders and tossed it away. He took the silky camisole and guided it up, over her head. He tossed that away, too, and put his big, warm hands against her rib cage, up tight under her breasts, lifting....

His mouth swooped down and captured a nipple, sucking it in, his tongue swirling around it. She speared her fingers through his hair, throwing her head back on a moan, holding those pleasuring lips tight against her, moving her hips along the rigid length of him, the lovely friction driving her wild.

He pulled back from her breast and looked at her, his eyes heavy-lidded, his mouth swollen and wet. "Let's go to bed." He slid forward on the chair. She curled her arms around his neck and he stood, his hands lifting her, settling her against him. "Wrap your legs around me...."

She hooked her sandaled feet behind him. They kissed as he carried her across the room. When they reached the curtain, she stuck out an arm to push it out of the way. In the small space beyond, there was the bed, a nightstand, and another curtain against the added-on side wall, masking off a closet of sorts.

Beau carried her to the bed and gently laid her down. The space had no window and the light that bled in from the main room was minimal. Starr reached over and turned on the bedside lamp.

They undressed, fast, unzipping and unbuttoning and tossing things away with wild abandon, all the while looking into each other's eyes. Naked at last, he stood before her at the edge of the bed.

She rose to her knees and took his hand—and then hesitated, admiring him. He was all lean, work-hardened muscle, broad in the shoulders, narrowing down to that tight, ridged belly. Instead of pulling him onto the bed with her, she scooted closer, pressing herself against him, feeling his warmth, excited all the more by the differences between her own softness and his strength.

His manhood stood up, straining, fully erect against her stomach. She couldn't resist sliding a hand in, wrapping it around him. He twitched in her grip and she giggled in delighted surprise.

Oh, he was so…silky. So silky and thick…

He groaned and pumped his hips against her. She experimented, grasping him fully and sliding her hand up—and then down the length of him.

He said her name, low, on a guttural moan. She looked up at him, watching his face, moving her hand on him, up and down, very slowly….

He grabbed her shoulders. "Wait…" It came out on a groan.

Shameless as always with him, she grinned. And she held on. Firmly. She felt him kick once more. Flushed with excitement and a lovely newfound sense of sexual power, she went on stroking him….

His fingers, still at her shoulders, dug in a little. "Just wait," he commanded through gritted teeth.

With a reluctant sigh, she let go. He released her shoulders and bent to scoop up his Wranglers, feeling in a front pocket and pulling out three small packets.

She might have been a virgin until a week ago, but

she'd been to health class. She'd seen the ads in magazines. She'd even had a couple of girlfriends at C.U. who carried packets like those in their purses at all times. Condoms.

She sank back to her knees and put her hands over her mouth. "Oh. Guess I should have thought of that...."

He dropped the jeans to the floor again. "You make me crazy, you know that?" His hot gaze ran over her.

She rested her hands on her knees—flagrantly pressing her breasts together with her arms—and slanted him a hopeful smile. "That's good, I hope?"

"We've got to be careful." Now he was looking extremely severe. The fact that lower down he was still hard as a fence post made her cover her mouth again to keep from letting out a silly giggle. "You think it's funny?" he demanded. Clearly, he didn't.

She composed herself. "Sorry. It's just...you look so stern. And yet, well, not *that* stern..."

"Starr, we have to face facts. We can't afford for you to get pregnant."

Her urge to laugh vanished. "I know that."

"I really blew it, that first time." His expression had softened. Regret shadowed his eyes. "I could shoot myself for that."

"Don't blame yourself. Please. We'll be careful from now on." Shyly, she held out her hand.

He set two of the condoms on the nightstand and slid the third beneath the pillow nearest him. Then at last, he let her pull him onto the bed with her. They stretched out on their sides, facing each other.

She stroked his hair, traced the shape of a golden

brow. "I'm sorry I made a joke of it. I know it's no joke, I do...."

He touched her shoulder, first with the pads of his fingers, then with his palm. He brushed it, that palm, back and forth against her skin, a caress that tantalized and teased.

"When I'm with you," he whispered, "it's too damn easy to forget the precautions."

"I'll help you remember. I promise I will." She kept her eyes open, looked straight at him, though she wanted to let them drift shut, to get lost in the wonder of the two of them, here, together. At last.

He gave her his slow smile, his brushing palm moving downward along her arm. At her elbow, he transferred his attention to her waist, clasping it, as if testing the shape of that inward curve, then tracing the slope of her hip, coming to rest at the topmost swell. His thumb brushed the ladybug. "You never told me how you got this...." Her breath caught at the feel of his thumb so close to the place she was wishing he might touch. That thumb brushed back and forth. It was maddening. In a thoroughly delightful way. "Tell me," he whispered.

"Now?" Really, she would have very much preferred to concentrate on what his thumb was doing.

His fingers moved a fraction closer to where she longed for them to be. "Now's as good a time as any." His touch moved lower still.

She gasped. "That's assuming..."

"What?"

"Assuming I can talk..."

"Give it your best shot." He cupped her.

"Oh!"

"Yeah?"

"Beau…"

"Tell me."

"I…"

"Yeah?"

"I was…fifteen…"

"And?"

She moved her hips toward him, let her thighs part just the slightest little bit. And then she moaned. "I…ran away, for the fifth or sixth time…from my mother, in San Diego. I…went with some friends who were…about as messed up as I was. I…oh!"

"Yeah?"

"Mexican tattoo parlor." She groaned. "On a dare…" She reached out and wrapped her hand around the back of his neck. Through gritted teeth, she demanded, "Happy now?"

"Oh, yeah." He kissed her. And down there between her slightly parted thighs, his knowing fingers continued their maddening play.

Urging her over onto her back, he canted up on an elbow beside her, lifting his mouth from hers—only to lower it to her breast. He sucked the nipple in. His fingers kept up their magic dance, sliding along every secret, wet fold, slipping inside….

She cried out and lifted her hips off the bed. He muttered something low and hot and needful. And then he took that tormenting hand away. He reached under the pillow and got out the condom, quickly dispensing with the wrapping, sliding it on over himself.

And then he was rising above her, settling himself between her parted thighs. He braced his elbows on the mattress, supporting the upper half of his body.

She smiled a little at that. It was so like him, to be careful not to crush her beneath him. His hands were pressed to the mattress, her hair spilling over them. He tangled his fingers into the black strands.

She felt him, there, the silky head nudging her. Staring into his eyes, she reached down and guided him.

"Slow," he whispered, the sound so needful, his breath coming ragged, warm across her cheek. "Careful…"

She was very wet. And ready—or so she thought.

Still, her body tightened against him. It hurt—just a little. But he was so gentle, entering by slow degrees, holding himself in check each time he pushed in a little more, waiting for her to relax and accept him. She strained her head up, hungry for his kiss.

He gave it, his mouth closing over hers, a groan rising from his throat as she took him in—a long, slow, ever-deepening slide.

And then, at last, she had all of him. She moaned into his mouth.

He lifted his head, fingers tightening in her hair. "Shh. Starr. It's okay, it's all right…just…please. Don't move.…"

Forever hung on a heartbeat. They stayed like that, so still, locked together for the longest time. Slowly, the tightness subsided. She felt herself opening, growing eager again.

She squirmed beneath him, wanting…more. "Beau. Oh, please…"

He began to move, a slow, rocking motion. Instinctively, she raised her legs and locked them around him.

The wonder began. She held on tight, taking her

cues from him, pressing herself so close, meeting each thrust.

Oh, it was happening—that gathering sensation. It spread out in ripples, upward, down and out...until ever inch of her vibrated with pleasure. She rolled her head on the pillow, moving with him, calling out his name as that wonderful, soft pulsing began.

Chapter Eight

Beau came to her at the cabin at least three times a week. He couldn't come every night—after all, he did have to get up to work every day before dawn.

Starr invented ways to see him more often. She carried meals over to Daniel's place—sometimes at midday, sometimes in the evening—and the three of them ate together.

Daniel praised her cooking. She called him an old flatterer and he beamed in pleasure, as if she'd granted him the highest of compliments. She really was becoming so fond of the old guy.

The first weekend in August, Tess threw a family barbecue. They set up a couple of canopies out in the yard and put two long threshing tables together and they all sat outside to eat slow-cooked ribs—and steaks and burgers, too.

The cousins came—Nate and Cash Bravo—with their wives and children. The three Bravo cousins owned the Rising Sun jointly. Nate lived and worked on his wife Meggie's ranch nearby. Cash and his wife Abby and their two sons had a house in town. Cash was an entrepreneurial type, always making some deal or other—and successful at it, too. Abby, who was Edna's daughter, managed the money Cash made.

Starr always got a kick out of seeing Abby and Edna together. The love between them was obvious, but still, they tended to get on each other's nerves. Edna did like to run things. And Abby was a woman who refused to be run. Edna was a portrait in womanly virtues; she could whip up a home-cooked meal with one hand tied behind her back. She liked things neat and tidy and she loved to sew. Like Tess, she could sit for hours making baby clothes or doing the mending, each stitch a marvel, tiny and perfect as the next. Abby, who worked hard managing her husband's investments and raising her boys, would order takeout instead of cooking; if a sock needed mending, she'd toss it in the trash and buy another pair. She got zero satisfaction from all the details of running a house. She had a cook/housekeeper—which, if you asked Edna, was a "needless extravagance."

Daniel also came to the family party—and Beau, too. Starr and Beau sat together when it came time to eat. Once, Beau's leg brushed hers and she sent him a questioning look. He only smiled his slow smile—and brushed her leg a second time.

Funny, how sometimes a random moment will snag on your heart and you know you will treasure it always. That moment was one of those. With her family all around them, and Edna and Abby arguing over whether Abby's toddler should be allowed to have a pacifier, Starr and Beau shared a private look. Surrounded by all those Bravos, they were, at the same time, the only two people on earth.

The night of the barbecue, after he took Daniel home, Beau came back to see her at the cabin. He hung his hat on the hook by the door, swept her into his arms and carried her to bed.

A little later, as they lay there all wrapped up together, he said how much it meant to him, just to be around her family. "Before you Bravos," he said, "I never saw a real family up close. I never believed, deep down, that there could even be such a thing, kin who...took care of each other, who all worked together to make a better life..."

Once, the Tisdales had owned a pretty good spread. His father, Beau said, had drunk it all away. Tyler Tisdale liked his whisky more than he ever cared for anything—including his wife and his three sons. "He had his whisky and his cruel and crooked little heart and that was all he needed...."

Beau talked about his mom that night. His voice was soft when he spoke of her, soft and so sad. "She was a good woman. Gentle, you know? My dad would beat on her and she would...bear it. She wore long sleeves and high collars in summer to cover the bruises."

Starr couldn't understand how Beau's mother had put up with so much abuse. "She should have left him."

"She did leave him, once. Took me with her, down to Arkansas where my grandmother lived. Fat lot of good it did her to try to escape him. My dad just came and got us and when he had her alone, at home…'' He didn't finish that sentence. ''She never tried to leave again. And she died of pneumonia a few years later. By then, my brothers were in their teens—a couple of mean, ugly-hearted chips off the old block. They would beat on her, too. Sometimes I think she died just to get away from them.''

At least, Starr thought, there was *some* justice in the world. ''They got theirs, those brothers of yours.''

''Yeah…'' The word kind of trailed off, filled with regret. He was staring up, into nothing, and she sensed that he might have said more.

She touched his square jaw and he turned his head to look at her. ''What?'' she asked softly.

''I just…should've stood up to them more.'' He gave a dry, humorless chuckle. '''Course, every time I did, they'd knock me right down and cut me with something. Or burn me. T.J. was the one who loved to burn me. Lyle'd hold me down and T.J.'d have that cigarette ready…'' He let out a hard gust of breath. ''My dad taught them good. They knew not to get me on the face. Cuts and burns and bruises on the body can be covered up with clothing. But who's gonna buy it if you go around with something covering your head? Uh-uh. People are bound to notice if you're cut up on the face. They would've had the police or the child protective services people down on them for that.…''

He fell silent again. And then, in a faraway voice, as if he was talking to himself more than to her, he said, ''Over the years, it got to be like they *owned* me.

They kind of...took me over, cut by cut and burn by burn."

She cuddled in tight to him, pressing her lips to a burst of scar tissue at his shoulder. "But you did stand up to them—in the end."

"Not soon enough," he said, and then, as if to emphasize the point, he said it again. "Not soon enough...and they were the ones who blew it there."

She tipped her head back to look at him. "How?"

"By making me go to work for your dad as part of their scheme to rustle Rising Sun cattle. I met your dad—and liked him from the first. I sat down to eat in the kitchen with your family...and I met you. I started thinking the wildest thoughts. That if you could care about me, maybe I should care a little more about myself. That there were people in the world who led clean, honest lives. That I would give just about anything for a chance to live like that myself."

Much later that night, Beau lay in Starr's bed, awake.

He watched Starr as she slept. She looked so soft and trusting.

He wished he could sleep like that, careless and easy, all the worries of the world pushed away.

But he never could. There was always, for him, a certain level he stayed at. A level of readiness, he supposed. Any odd, meaningless noise—the wind in the eaves, a coyote's cry—could bring him right up to full alertness.

He kissed her temple. She only sighed and snuggled closer. He brushed her hair away from her forehead. "Starr..."

"Hmm?" She opened one eye, grinned—and then stretched.

"Gotta go."

"No…"

"Yeah."

"Stay. Just for a little while…" She stuck out her lower lip, pretending to pout.

He resisted the urge to kiss that pout away. "Sorry." He eased his arm out from under her, sat up and swung his legs to the floor.

Starr lay back on her pillow and watched him dress, admiring the play of muscles in his back as he pulled on his jeans and his boots. The white scars where there, too. But not so thick as on his chest. He grabbed his shirt and stuck his arms in it, standing as he started buttoning up, turning to give her a smile.

She asked, "Give me my robe, will you?"

He lifted it from its peg and she got up and tied it around her and walked him to the door. He kissed her there, on the threshold. She clung a little, but surrendered to his leaving when he took her by the shoulders and gently set her away. He reached for his hat.

She smiled to herself at that, a woman's knowing smile. "When a man reaches for his hat, a girl knows there's no keeping him.…"

He touched her chin, tipping it up, and brushed one last kiss against her lips. "You know I'll be back."

She stood in the doorway and watched him go, wishing that, just one time, he could stay till dawn.

He waved as he drove away. She waved back, feeling dreamy and content—and yet, still, a little bit sad.

When his taillights disappeared in the night, she shut the door and went back to bed. She switched off the light and lay there alone, listening to a coyote howling somewhere out in the darkness.

A second howl joined the first and that made her feel better, somehow, more at peace with the way the things were between her and Beau. They didn't have forever. He didn't even spend the whole night.

But still, this was a beautiful time, this summer of theirs. It was perfect, in its way.

A few nights later, as they lay there in bed, a storm came up. The rain beat on the old roof and it felt so good, just to lie there with Beau's cherishing arms holding her close, listening to it coming down—until they realized there was a dripping sound coming from the outer room.

Buck naked, they jumped out of bed to investigate and discovered a leak in the roof, above the iron day-bed that sat against the far wall. Laughing together, they shoved the bed out of the way and Starr found a bucket to catch the drips.

"I'll get Tim to look at the roof tomorrow," she told him. They went back to bed. Around midnight, as always, he took his leave.

She woke in the morning to the sound of someone hammering up on the roof. She went out into the clear sunlight and the muddy yard to find Beau up there, fixing the leak. When he came down, she gave him coffee and told him she'd decided to keep him around.

He pulled her into his lap and kissed her soundly. "You've made the right decision, as I am yours for the whole summer. You'd have a hell of a time getting rid of me before Labor Day."

She felt a little stab of sadness and she couldn't keep herself from asking, "Only for the summer?"

He must have noticed the change in her tone. He said, quietly, "Yeah. For the summer. That was the deal."

She laid her hand on the side of his face, felt the roughness of morning stubble—and wondered how she would bear it when September came around. "Right. That was the deal." She gave him a smile and another long kiss and he left a few minutes later.

Starr watched him drive off and reminded herself that she had a job lined up in New York, a job she wanted that would lead to a better job. In a year, she'd be an assistant editor. She planned to work hard and keep focused and move up the ranks quickly. She'd be a full-fledged editor in no time. She wasn't walking away from her own future—and Beau didn't *want* her to walk away from it.

That day, her period was due. It didn't come. She hardly gave it a thought.

But a week later, when her period still hadn't come, she found herself thinking about it often. By then, the worry had become a constant nagging in the back of her mind.

Beau came over that night, a Tuesday. They had chicken-fried steak with country gravy and after the meal, they spent a long, sweet time making love.

When he got up to go, he asked if something was bothering her. "You seem…I don't know. Kind of far away. You got something on your mind?"

She almost told him her fears right then. But no, she decided. Better find out for certain before laying something like this on the poor guy. So she lied. She reassured him there was nothing and sent him on his way.

After he was gone, she sank back among the pillows with a sigh and admitted to herself that it was time she found out for certain. She needed a home pregnancy test—and she didn't want to buy it at the drugstore in Medicine Creek.

Okay, maybe she was being paranoid, but she could run into anyone in there. People seemed to be pretty much minding their own business when it came to her and Beau. But it *was* a small town. If someone who liked to gossip saw her buying a kit, it could get back to Beau—and her dad and Tess—before she even had a chance to take the darn thing. Then what?

The test would probably turn out negative. Why get everyone upset if there really wasn't anything to be upset about?

She could go on over to Buffalo....

But no. Even going there made her nervous. Her family was locally so well-known; someone *might* recognize her. And Sheridan wasn't all that much farther away than Buffalo, really....

Oh, she was being stupid, and she knew it. Women did get pregnant, after all. It was a fact of life. So what if some casual acquaintance happened to see her buying a test? What did she care?

A lot, she thought. *I care a lot.* Not for herself so much, but there *was* her dad. Zach Bravo might turn a blind eye to the way Beau's pickup was parked in front of the cabin till midnight most nights. But if Starr turned up pregnant, he was not going to be happy.

Not until Beau had married her...

And even more important than her dad's reaction, there was Beau himself. If she was having Beau's baby, he had a right to hear the news first from her own lips—not from some town tale-teller.

Wednesday, she had to work with Jerry from eight to five, putting the paper to bed for the week. She headed for Sheridan as soon as she got off.

It took less than half an hour to get there from town. She found a Kmart on North Main and bought the test without recognizing a soul. She was back in the Suburban and on her way home before six, turning into the drive that led to the ranch house—and her own place beyond it—by six forty-five.

She saw Beau's pickup, there in the clear space in front of the cabin, as she drove in. He was waiting on the step. He rose as she pulled to a stop.

The bag with the test in it sat on the passenger seat in plain view. She snatched it up and stuck it under her own seat without even thinking twice. No need for him to see it—and maybe ask her what was in it.

He strode to her door and pulled it open for her. "Working late, huh?"

She lied by evasion. "What a day—but if I'd known you were coming over, I'd have told Jerry I couldn't stay."

He reached out a hand to help her down, then hooked an arm around her waist. The familiar thrill went through her, as he pulled her close. His eyes gleamed down at her and his strong arms held her as if he would never let her go. "Why is it I can't seem to keep away from you?"

She stretched up and kissed his handsome nose.

"Do you hear me complaining?" *Tomorrow,* she thought. *I'll tell him tomorrow.*

Once she knew for certain that it was a false alarm, she'd tell him how worried she'd been. They would laugh about it, about how it had been a close call and she'd gotten so freaked over it, she'd hid the test from him and lied about her trip to Sheridan. They would say how they really had nothing to worry about. They'd been so careful, except for that first time.

And then, in a day or two, her period would come....

Oh, yes. She was sure of it. It was going to be all right.

He kissed her—a long, sweet kiss. When he raised his head, she grabbed his hand. "Come on. Let's see what we can find to eat around here."

In the morning, first thing, she went out and got the bag from under the seat. She took the test in the bathroom out back.

When she looked at the result panel, her mouth went dry as prairie dust and her heart stopped beating—then started up again, triple-time. Her hands felt sweaty and a hot flush flooded upward over her cheeks.

It was not all right, after all. She did, very definitely, have something to worry about.

Chapter Nine

Beau didn't come to see her that night—and she didn't drive over to Daniel's to see him. She wasn't ready yet to talk about it. Not with Beau—not with anyone.

Friday, they'd planned a night out: Carmelita's for dinner, and then maybe over to Mustang Sally's for a couple of beers and a dance or two. But when he arrived to pick her up, she told him she'd rather just stay home.

He didn't care if they went out or not, so she fixed a simple dinner and they strolled down by the creek and later they made slow, sweet love.

She was thinking she would tell him her problem then, after the loving, while they were lying there, all content and relaxed in each other's arms.

But the right words, somehow, just wouldn't come. And then he tipped her chin up and kissed her again.

She gave herself up to his kiss, to his touch. For a while, lost in his arms, she forgot all about the little problem she had.

Saturday, she went over to the main house to work for a while. She made several calls to various neighbors, found out who was visiting whom; who was planning a trip, and where they would go. Then she sat down at her computer to write Mabel Ruby's column, Over The Back Fence.

Mabel was in her nineties. She'd been writing the column for forty years and telling Jerry for the last five of those years that she wanted to retire.

Jerry wouldn't hear of it. "People count on you, Mabel. They want to know what's going on with their neighbors—who took a trip to California, whose great-uncle Harold is staying for the week...."

Since he wouldn't let her quit officially, Mabel just stopped turning in the columns. Jerry wrote them for her—or had Starr do it during the summer.

Starr wrote, *Bobby Terry's back in town from Boston for a short vacation, staying with the Terry family at the Terry Ranch.* Rumor had it Bobby's wife had kicked him out again—but of course, Over The Back Fence wouldn't include any news like that.

As she wrote, Starr took care never to give specific dates for when people would be out of town. Ten years back, some local lowlife had caught on to watching the column for times when folks would be away. He'd made a tidy haul, breaking in and burglarizing their empty houses—until he got caught and confessed how he'd known which houses to rob.

Faith and Kevin Johnston have bought a new pop-up vacation trailer. They'll be hitting the road soon

*for a two-week trip to the Pacific Northwest with
daughters Kim, 7, and Kaylee, 9.* Over the phone,
Faith had confided she was pregnant again. "Just between you and me, Starr..."

Pregnant, Starr thought. The word kind of stalled
her out. She stared blankly at the screen for a while.

Lucky Faith, with a loving husband and two little
girls and a pop-up vacation trailer. Faith was at that
place in her life where a baby made total sense....

Starr took a break, joining Tess and Edna in the
kitchen where they were preparing the midday meal.
Edna stood at the stove frying sausage and ground
beef. Spaghetti sauce bubbled on the back burner.
Tess, at the counter, spread her special butter and gar-
lic paste onto split loaves of French bread. Ethan sat
at the table with a coloring book and crayons.

"Starr, c'mere," her brother commanded. "Look."
He pointed at a row of stick figures he'd drawn.
"Mommy and Daddy and Auntie Ed. And you and
Jo...and Reggie." He made a sad face. Zach's old
hound had died that past winter. "See?" He pointed
at the crooked halo he'd drawn above the stick-dog's
head. "He's just visiting. From heaven." He pointed
at the smallest figure. "And that's me. Cute, huh?"

"Very." She ruffled his hair.

"Cut it out," he grumbled, ducking away from her
affectionate hand. "Can't you see I'm *busy?*"

Starr stared down at his bent head, at his little hand
wrapped around a red crayon....

Hadn't it only been yesterday that he was teething?
He'd held up his little arms to her. "Stah, Stah..."
Starr had got him a teething biscuit and sat out on the

front porch with him in her arms, rocking him until he dropped off to sleep.

Now, here he was, almost five, big enough to be insulted when she ruffled his hair. He'd be heading off to school in no time. How had this happened?

Tess was talking to her. "Feel like cutting up a salad?"

Starr blinked. "Uh. Sure." She got the greens and the other stuff from the fridge and hauled it all to the sink. She pulled the big wooden salad bowl down from the shelf, got out a cutting board and a nice, sharp knife and set to work.

Tess had the bread ready. At the last minute, she'd pop it in the oven. Tidy as always, she began cleaning up her work area. "'Scuse me."

Starr ducked away as she opened a cupboard. Her pink shirt rode up and Starr got a quick glimpse of the front of her jeans.

Unsnapped.

Pregnant, Starr thought, as if she didn't already know. *Pregnant.* The word itself seemed to have new layers of meaning—all them scary. Soon Tess would be wearing those stretch jeans with the pregnancy panel. She'd get big as Meggie was now. Wherever she went, her stomach would lead the way.

And then, in January, there'd be a new baby.

Her mind only half focused on the action, Starr brought the knife down. Instead of the radish on the board, she cut a big slice out of her finger. The blood welled up, a red so dark it almost looked black. Starr stared at it, appalled.

Tess was right there. "Oh, no. Here." She flipped

on the faucet. "Better give me that." She took the knife.

Over at the stove, Edna clucked her tongue. "Is it bad?"

"Just a nasty little slice," said Tess. She had Starr by the wrist and guided her hand under the running tap. They both watched the blood well, the stream of water wash it away. Tess gave her smile. "Better?"

Starr watched the pink-tinted water as it spun down the drain, wondering at the way life could suddenly get away from a person. You turned around and your brother was just about five, for crying out loud. And your stepmother was pregnant, just like Meggie and Faith Johnston....

Just like me....

"Starr?" Tess was looking at her with a puzzled, slightly worried frown. "Is something the matter?"

The smell of the cooking meat, of the bubbling spaghetti sauce... God. She could not deal with it. "Could you...get me a paper towel?" Tess tore off a towel from the roll hooked under the cabinet. "Thanks." Starr wrapped her still-bleeding finger in it. "I think I'd better—" she paused to swallow the sudden nausea down "—get a Band-Aid..." Holding the towel around her finger, Starr made for the stairs.

"Wait," Tess called. "There's a Band-Aid right here in the—"

Starr didn't pause—she didn't dare. She turned and walked backward, holding her towel-wrapped, bleeding finger high. "I'd better go upstairs. Finish the salad for me?"

"Of course, but—"

Whatever else she said, Starr didn't stick around to

hear it. She whirled and bolted for the stairs, taking them two at a time, racing for the bathroom at the end of the upper hall.

Once she got in there, she shoved the door closed, twisted the privacy lock, knocked the lid shut on the toilet—Ethan was always leaving it up—and dropped to the seat.

Still holding the towel around her finger, she put her head between her knees and sucked in a series of slow, calming breaths—all the while half expecting Tess to tap on the door and ask if she was okay.

No tap came. And the feeling that she was going to chuck up what was left of her breakfast was passing.

Still hunched over, she braced her elbows on her knees and studied the bloody towel that covered her finger. "Oh, what am I gonna do?" she whispered to the empty bathroom.

Not surprisingly, no one answered.

An abortion?

No. She just…didn't want to do that. She put her uncut hand against her flat stomach and thought of how she'd be wearing preggie-panel stretch jeans herself in a few months. She shut her eyes and counted.

April. If nothing went wrong, in April, she'd be having her baby. It seemed such a long way away.…

And at the same time, it seemed like tomorrow. She'd have her baby and…he'd grow up too fast. Like Ethan. She'd turn around one day and he'd be sitting at the table, drawing pictures, complaining if she ruffled his hair.

Life was so strange. She stared down at the tiles between her feet, picking out the patterns in the spaces between. You could start out a summer on one road…

And end up somewhere altogether different than where you thought you were going.

"Beau?" she whispered.

It was a good question. What about Beau? She really *would* have to tell him. Soon.

And when she did…

Well, did she want to marry him?

God. Where would they live?

New York had *doubtful* written all over it. He wouldn't want to go there in the first place—and what would he *do* if he did? There weren't a lot of ranches to run in Manhattan.

So then. Say, just for the sake of argument, that she accepted the fact Beau wasn't a New York kind of guy and decided to stay here, in Wyoming, with him.

Was she ready to be a rancher's wife?

Starr straightened. She felt better. The nausea was gone.

A rancher's wife?

Well, okay. Yeah. Maybe she was.

Maybe she *loved* him.

She grinned at the sink across from her. Oh, hell. She *did* love him. She'd loved him forever, even when she was telling herself she hated him. She'd loved him from the first moment they set eyes on each other, when he stood up in the back of that pickup and put his hat over his heart.

Yeah, okay. It was romantic and foolish. Some would even say impossible…

But then again, why wouldn't they be able to make it as a couple?

And who said she had to leave home to find herself a job?

So much was done by computer nowadays. She could get freelance work. And she could take Jerry up on that offer of a permanent job.

And money was no issue, anyway. Her dad and Tess liked the ranching life. They lived simply, way below their means. But there was plenty they could draw on if they ever needed it. The Rising Sun Cattle Company turned a tidy profit nearly every year. And her dad had inherited a fortune from Grandmother Elaine's side of the family. Starr herself had a nice, fat trust fund.

She and Beau could build a place of their own out there at the Hart ranch. She had a feeling Daniel would say yes to that in the blink of an eye. And until the house was finished, they could make do at Daniel's. He had plenty of room—and if Daniel wasn't up to having a couple of newlyweds underfoot, fine. They could live in Beau's trailer. It would only be for a little while, after all.

The point was, they *could* do it. Get married. Start a life together. They'd have as good a chance as lots of other couples at making it work. Maybe a *better* chance. It wasn't as if they'd just met this summer, as if they'd been strangers until a few weeks ago. She'd been in love with him for six years.

And though he'd never said it, she was pretty certain he felt the same about her.

Starr got up and went to the medicine cabinet. She threw the bloodstained paper towel away, took down the box of adhesive strips, and wrapped a strip around her finger—dayglow-green, printed with arching black cats. Ethan demanded bright colors and animal prints on his adhesive strips.

The tap on the door came as she was putting the box of bandages away. "Starr?" It was Tess, sounding worried. "Are you all right?"

Starr shut the medicine cabinet door and called, "I'm fine." And she was, now she knew what she would do.

Now, if she could just figure out the best way to tell Beau…

After the midday meal, when her dad and Jobeth and the hands had gone back out to work and the dishes were cleaned up, Starr helped Edna put a pot roast on for dinner. Then Edna took Ethan across the yard to her place for an hour and Starr returned to her computer to finish Mabel's column. Tess came up, too, for a rest. She was feeling a little tired, she said.

The old house was quiet, except for Starr's fingers tapping the computer keys. *Carmen Amestoy's Aunt Alberta Carr is here from Canada. "Aunt Alberta just loves Bighorn Country in summer," Carmen reports. "She wants to catch the Lions Club rodeo over at the fairgrounds and she never misses the—"*

"Starr?"

It was Tess, standing in the doorway, her face dead white except for two fevered spots of color high on her cheeks. She had a hand over her stomach. And her jeans were…darker, a spreading stain, along the insides of her thighs.

"Starr…" Tess staggered and clutched the door frame for support. "I was just lying there, and I felt something give. I… Oh, dear God. I think something's gone wrong…."

Chapter Ten

Starr led Tess to the bed, helped her to lie down and then dialed 911.

"They're sending the helicopter out for you," she promised as she hung up. "They'll call Doc Pruitt for us." Tess moaned, her hand pressing her belly. The stain kept getting bigger, creeping down her legs, spreading wider.... "Should we do something? Try to stop the bleeding?"

Tess was panting now. "No stopping it." She cried out, drawing her legs up into a tight fetal press. She moaned. "Oh, God. Your father..."

"I'll get him on that phone he keeps in the truck."

Tess groaned out the number and Starr punched it up. She heard the ringing, and then the canned voice informing her that no one was available to answer her call. "No answer..." she replied to the frantic question in Tess's eyes. She waited for the beep and left a rattled message. "Dad, it's Starr. Tess is having problems. She was…resting and she started bleeding…" Tess reached out, groping for a steadying hand. Starr's was the only hand available. She gave it. Tess crushed her fingers as she cried out again. Starr bore the grinding grip and spoke into the phone. "Dad, they're sending the EMT helicopter over. You better get back here to the house as quick as you can." She hung up as Tess shot to a sitting position.

"Bathroom. Now. Help me…" Tess swung her feet to the floor and bolted upright, then almost collapsed before Starr got her under the arms.

"Hold on, hold on. We're going…" She hauled Tess's arm across her shoulder. "Lean on me. It's okay…"

Okay… What a ludicrous thing to say. It wasn't. Not okay in the least. They staggered out the door and along the upper hall, headed for the closest bathroom, the one near the top of the stairs. "Come on, you'll make it, we're almost there…" Starr whispered encouragements while inside she cursed every reeling step between them and their destination.

They reached the bathroom at last. Starr helped Tess get the wet jeans down, biting back a cry of alarm at the sight of the blood-soaked white panties underneath. Tess stumbled to the toilet, Starr supporting her, helping her to lower herself to the seat.

Tess moaned, wrapping her arms around herself, hunching over so her head touched her knees. "There's nothing…I thought…"

What to say? How to help? "Just…relax…just try

to breathe as slow and even as you can." Starr thought, *I'll call Edna*. Edna would know what to do.

But Tess grabbed her hand again. "Don't leave me. Oh, God. Don't leave me alone…"

What could she say, but, "I won't. I swear. I'm right here…"

Tess ground even harder on Starr's hand. "It's not…I thought…"

Starr moved in closer. "I'm here. Hold on…"

"Oh, Starr…" With an anguished sigh, Tess rested her head against Starr's side.

"I'm here. Right here with you…" She stroked Tess's brown curls and prayed silently, *Please, God. Oh, please, please make this stop….*

But it didn't stop. Tess groaned and mangled Starr's hand and muttered between moans, "It hurts…oh, my baby…oh, hold on…help is coming…"

It went on forever—Tess in such agony, one minute talking to her baby, the next just bent over, moaning in pain. There was more blood—too much blood, it seemed to Starr. The coppery smell of it filled the small room. But it didn't look like Tess had lost the baby.

At least, not yet…

"Oh, hurry," Tess kept moaning. "Oh, please, make them come…"

Perhaps fifteen never-ending minutes after they reached the bathroom, Starr heard the sound of helicopter blades chopping the air. She knelt in front of Tess. "Tess. Tess, do you hear it? They're here. They're out in front…."

Tess looked at her through wide, terrified eyes. "Oh, get them," she cried, her pretty heart-shaped face stark white, contorted with pain. "Get them up here now."

"I will." Tess still clutched her hand in a death grip. "Tess," she said softly. "Tess, you have to let go…"

Tess held on all the harder. "Oh, no. Don't leave. You can't leave."

Terrified herself, Starr stared into those glazed brown eyes. The world seemed turned upside down at that moment. For years, it had been Tess she leaned on, Tess she could trust with her secrets and her plans.

Now it was all turned around. Tess needed *her*. Now Starr must be strong and determined for both of them. She didn't want to leave Tess any more than her stepmother wanted her to go—not even for the time it would take to run downstairs and get those EMTs up here. But someone had to go….

"Okay," she whispered, stroking Tess's hair. "We'll wait till they ring the bell, all right? Then I'll have to go down and get them."

"Yes. Yes, all right." Tess groaned and hunched low again.

Starr held her hand and rubbed her back. "Just a minute, just a minute now, they'll be here…." After another eternity, the doorbell rang. "There…" But Tess only let out a panicked cry and gripped Starr's hand all the harder. "Tess, please. I'll be back. I'll be back in no time at all…."

With a groan, Tess released her. "Go, go…"

Starr raced out into the hall and pounded down the stairs. When she flung open the front door, two men in flight suits were standing there, each with a jump kit clutched in his hand. She'd never been so grateful to see anyone. The phone started ringing. Starr ignored it.

"This way," she said and led the two men up the stairs.

To Starr, things seemed to go by in a blur after that.

They put Tess on a stretcher and brought her down the stairs. Edna, who'd come on across the yard when no one answered her call, insisted on staying by Tess in the helicopter.

There was only so much room in there and someone had to stay with Ethan, but Starr couldn't bear to leave Tess's side. "I thought I would go with her…"

"No." Edna was white-faced, lips pressed together, her pointy chin at its most stubborn slant. "I think *I* should go."

"Better decide," warned one of the EMTs. "Fast."

In the end, the need in Edna's eyes was so achingly clear, Starr couldn't deny her. "Okay. You go. I'll look out for things here."

"Zach…Ethan…" Tess moaned as they were lifting her into the helicopter.

"I'll take good care of Ethan," Starr promised. "And I'll get hold of Dad. I'll keep trying till I reach him."

Edna grabbed Starr in a quick hug. "Check on the little one right away. He was still napping when I ran out."

"I will."

"And don't let him see that mess in the bathroom."

For once, she was grateful for Edna's never-ending advice. "You're right. I didn't even think about that.…"

"Mrs. Heller. We have to go."

Edna held out her hand and the technician helped her in. He jumped in himself. Starr stepped back as the big blades started turning. The machine lifted into the sky, blowing up dirt devils. Starr squinted through the swirling dust, using her hand as a visor. As the white-bellied aircraft curved off to the north, she sent along another silent, heartfelt prayer for the safe return of Tess and her baby.

When she lowered her gaze, Ethan was running toward her across the yard. "Starr! Starr, was that a 'copter?"

She forced a wide smile. "You bet it was."

He launched himself at her. She caught him, hoisting him up, with his strong little legs squeezing either side of her waist. He laughed—and then shoved at her shoulder. "Put me down—I'm too big to be carried."

So she set him down and he scolded her, "Where's Auntie Ed? And why didn't you wake me up if a 'copter was coming?"

She held down her hand and wiggled her fingers. With some reluctance, he grabbed her index finger. "Come on. Let's go on in the house. I have to make a few calls and you must be very good and quiet while I do that."

"Where's Mom?" He tipped his head at an angle, his eyes narrowed in suspicion.

Why was it that little kids always figured out more than they needed to know? "Mom had to go—in the helicopter. Auntie Ed went with her."

"Why?"

She knelt down in the dirt to get at eye level with him. "Mom's sick. They're taking her to the doctor."

"What's wrong with her?"

"She's sick," Starr said again, praying that this time he'd accept that as an explanation. "And they're taking her to the place where she can get well."

He looked very solemn now. "Starr. I want Mom."

"I know you do, honey. But she has to get well first."

The minute they got inside the house, Ethan announced he had to go to the bathroom. Starr ushered him into the downstairs half bath with a reminder to wash his hands when he was through. While he was in there, she checked the pot roast and then got busy fixing him a snack of graham crackers and milk.

She let him take the snack into the great room, even set up a tray for him and allowed him to sit in their dad's big easy chair. She turned on the TV and handed him the remote.

"Can I trust you with this?"

"Starr. I'm almost five."

She left him to his gleeful channel surfing and ran upstairs to wipe down the bathroom and gather up Tess's bloody clothes. When the evidence of what had happened there was all cleaned away, she checked on Ethan. He seemed content enough.

"I'll be in Dad's office if you need me."

"Ungh," he said, chewing a graham cracker, pointing the remote at the TV.

She went to the office off the dining room, shut the door behind her and speed-dialed her father's cell.

Again, no answer. She tried the Double K—Nate and Meggie's place—next. Nate and her dad often worked together, Meggie alongside them. But at eight and a half months pregnant, Meggie was keeping close to the house now.

Meggie had no more idea than Starr did as to where Zach might be. She promised to send Nate out to track him down, if her husband came in with any information.

Starr called Daniel's house. The old man was getting better every day, but he still wasn't working more than a few hours at stretch. He should be there....

"Hart Ranch." It was Beau's voice.

She hadn't expected him to answer. "Beau. Hi. It's me."

"Hey." His voice was warm. Intimate. Normal.

She gulped to relax her suddenly strangled throat. "What are you doing home?"

He said something about having a few things to pick up, coming in to fill up the cooler, then teased, "What? You'd rather talk to Daniel than to me?"

"No. No, I...it's just I..."

"Starr." His voice had gone flat. "What's the matter?"

She had an image of Tess, bent over, groaning, curly head on her knees, the white knuckles gripping... "I need to find my dad. I need to find him really bad. I called the cell he keeps in the pickup, but he didn't answer. I called Meggie at the Double K. She didn't know where to find him. Do you know where he is?"

A pause, then he said, "I just left him fifteen minutes ago."

Hope had her drawing herself up a little straighter. "So you can go get him? Tell him to get home right now?"

"Yeah, I'll go get him. What's going on?"

Relief exploded through her. "Oh, good. Good."

"Starr…"

She realized she hadn't told him. "I…"

"What's happened? Tell me…"

It was like a dam going, then. She told him in a flood of words. "It's Tess, she's having a miscarriage, I think. We got the EMTs and they took her out in a helicopter to Memorial in Sheridan and Edna went with her and Tess wants my dad, but I can't find him. Oh, Beau. She needs him and I can't find him…."

Beau took the dirt roads out to the Farley breaks at a speed that wasn't the least bit safe. He must have hit every rut along the way, the undercarriage slamming the ground and rattling, his head bopping the roof when he went over the worst ones. He ignored the possible damage to the old pickup and drove on.

He got up that last ridge and went barreling down into the small valley where smoke spiraled up from either end of the long stretch of clogged ditch.

Zach and Jobeth and a couple of hands ranged along the banks of the stream. One of the hands poured diesel fuel on a fresh section, while the other waited, ready with the spray tank, in case the fire got loose from the bank. Jobeth and Zach raked tumbleweeds into the water to be doused with fuel when the time came. It was a job usually done earlier in the year— and in the morning before the heat of the day. All their shirts were dark with sweat.

Beau lurched to a stop next to Zach's pickup, jumped out and headed for Zach. He walked fast, but in his mind he was balking, pulling back from the prospect of giving Zach the rotten news.

Zach saw him coming. He leaned on his rake and gave him a wave. "We're makin' good progress—and you look like someone just shot your best hunting dog...." His easy expression changed, became wary. "We got a problem?"

"I need a minute or two." Beau gestured with a toss of his head.

"Sure." Zach dropped his rake and followed Beau back to the pickups.

When they got there, Beau couldn't find the words. He took off his hat, beat it on his thigh.

"Speak up, son."

He sucked in a big breath of smoke-sharp air—and let it out hard. "Starr called while I was at Daniel's. She's looking for you. They just airlifted Tess over to Sheridan. Zach, damn it. I'm sorry. It looks like a miscarriage."

Zach fell back a step. In his face was a starkness, a sudden awful knowledge, like a man who'd just lost his footing at the edge of a cliff. "She's alive, right?"

"Yeah. She's alive."

"The baby?"

"I don't know. Starr said she didn't think Tess had lost it. But she said it...well, it didn't look so good."

"Ethan?"

"Starr's got him, over at your place. She said Edna went in the helicopter with Tess."

Zach swore. And then his fist shot out.

Somehow, Beau stood his ground, unflinching. He'd been punched a lot in his life, and if it would help Zach now to hit someone, Beau was more than ready to take the blow. Hell, he'd take a thousand blows for the sake of the man in front of him.

But Zach only grabbed his shoulder, as if to steady himself. Beau had a sick moment of bleak wonder at his own reaction. Still, after all this time, when a man's hand came toward him, he expected to get hit.

Zach squeezed his shoulder. "Look after things here?"

"Yeah, we'll finish up."

Zach's hand dropped away. He drew himself up. "Tell Jobeth what's going on?"

Beau slid his hat back on. "I'll do that."

"I'll be heading straight for Sheridan."

Shovels and rakes and gas cans were piled in the back of the Rising Sun truck. Beau grabbed his cooler and the two extra rakes he'd collected at Daniel's and had Zach take the green pickup. "And don't forget that cell phone of yours. You can call Starr to tell her you've gone to Sheridan—and call ahead to the hospital to find out what's going on there." Zach grabbed the phone, climbed into Beau's pickup and roared off.

Beau turned to see that Jobeth was coming his way. Time to pass out the bad news for the second time. The same kind of thing had gone on when Daniel had his heart attack, a never-ending cycle of gently explaining what was going on. When you hung around with folks who looked out for each other and something went wrong, there was a whole damn lot of explaining to do.

He thought of Starr, alone at the ranch house with Ethan. She hadn't sounded good on the phone. He hoped she was holding up okay. The need to see her face rose in him—a kind of burning ache.

Jobeth was standing in front of him. "Beau, where'd Dad go?"

Beau took off his hat again and started explaining.

Starr stood at the counter by the sink, mixing dough for drop biscuits, grateful to have a dinner to get on the table. At a time like this, it really helped to have something useful to do. She could hear the drone of the TV in the living room. Ethan had been in there for hours now, lounging in their dad's favorite chair, king of the remote. Starr would check on him every now and then, just to make sure he wasn't watching anything he shouldn't be. And yeah, she knew all that TV couldn't be good for him. When Edna found out she'd probably have a fit.

But this was one of those times when a kid watching too much TV seemed like the least of anyone's problems. Starr went to the fridge for the milk and when she passed the window, she spotted one of her dad's pickups rolling in. It pulled to a stop by the barn. The hands jumped from the bed and started unloading gas cans and shovels. Jobeth and Beau, faces soot-blackened and shirts dark with sweat, climbed from the cab. Beau went around to help unload. Jobeth headed straight for the back door. Starr set the milk on the counter and went to meet her.

When Starr came through from the pantry into the laundry room, Jo was pulling off her mud-caked boots. She looked up. "Starr." Her face kind of crumpled. Starr held out her arms. One boot still on, Jobeth hobbled over. Starr grabbed her tight.

"Oh, Starr…"

Starr stroked her sooty hair and rocked her gently

back and forth, as if she were still the skinny little kid she'd been when Starr first returned to the Rising Sun.

Finally, Jo asked, "Any news?"

Starr smoothed a few loose strands of hair behind her sister's dirty ear. "Dad called about twenty minutes ago. He's at the hospital. Tess is going to be all right...."

"And the baby?"

Starr bit her lip and shook her head. "Dad said she lost it."

"Oh, no..." Jo's mouth trembled.

Starr pulled her close again, rocked her some more and whispered, "At least your mom's okay...or she will be. She'll be home in a few days, it looks like. And there can be other babies."

Jobeth sniffed in Starr's ear. "The doctor said that?"

"Yeah."

Jo hugged Starr even tighter than before. "Oh, it's just so sad...."

"I know."

Sniffling and rubbing her nose with the heel of her hand, Jo pulled herself together. "God. I got dirt all over your shirt."

"It'll wash out."

"Where's Ethan?"

Starr almost smiled. "Follow the sound of the television."

Jo leaned against the dryer, hitched up her other boot, eased it off and dropped it by the first one. "I'll clean up—and give you some help with dinner."

"Thanks—oh, and get one of Dad's shirts for Beau,

will you? Leave it in Ethan's bathroom. He can take a shower in there.''

Jo sent her a sideways look. "Beau's coming in?"

The question surprised her. How could he not? "Well, yeah. Of course he is."

"I got the idea he was taking off. He was talking about borrowing the pickup, since Dad took his. I figured that means he's heading on back to Daniel's...."

Beau leaving now? How could he *leave?* A part of her had been waiting all through the awful afternoon for him, counting the seconds until she could see his face. "He is so not going to do that. I need him right here."

Jobeth shrugged. "Well, better go get him, then."

Starr rushed outside. Beau and the hands were still unloading. She waited impatiently out of the way as they finished the job.

"Dinner at six," she told the hands. They went off to their trailers to get cleaned up.

That left her and Beau standing by the tailgate. He lifted it and hitched it up. "You okay?" Beneath the shadow of his hat, under the layer of grime, his expression was hard to read—careful, maybe? Worried?

She wanted to launch herself at him. But she stayed where she was. "I've been a lot better."

"You hear from your dad?"

She repeated what she'd told Jobeth.

"Tough," he said, shaking his head. "But at least Tess'll be okay...."

She gave up on waiting for him to reach for her. "Beau Tisdale, if you don't put your arms around me pretty soon, I think I might scream."

He frowned and looked down at his sweat-dark shirt and dirty Wranglers. "I'm filthy."

"I don't give a damn." She swayed toward him— and he caught her. Those strong arms closed around her. She sighed and pressed close, breathing in the smell of smoke and sweat, finding comfort at last. "It was so awful," she whispered, holding on tight. "I thought I might lose her. Right upstairs, in the bathroom. I thought she might die and I couldn't do a thing about it...."

"Shh..." She felt his lips against her hair. "Shh..."

She shut her eyes, holding him tighter still, longing rising inside her—to whisper her secret. To take his hand and press it to her flat stomach and say...

Oh, God. Say what? *No,* she thought. *Bad idea. This is not the time.*

She lifted her head. "You can stay for dinner. It's pot roast and there's plenty."

He held her away a little. "I need to clean up...."

"You can do it here. Jo's digging up a clean shirt for you. And we've had sooty Wranglers at the kitchen table before—oh, and I'll call Daniel. He can come on over and eat with us, too."

"You don't need company now."

"Company? What are you talking about? You and Daniel are like family. You know that." He had the strangest look on his face—reluctant. "Please," she said. "It would mean so much to me, if you would stay...."

He hesitated. That hurt. But then he shrugged. "Lead me to that clean shirt."

* * *

After dinner, the hands left to feed the horses and then for their trailers. Jobeth, Daniel and Beau pitched in to clean up. Even Ethan helped to clear off.

Once the table and counters were clean and the dishwasher running, Daniel volunteered to play Go Fish with Ethan—always an interesting experience, as Ethan's little hands could hardly hold the cards and he still wasn't all that clear yet on the whole concept of rules. Jobeth headed for the great room to catch a favorite TV show.

Starr led Beau out to the front porch. They sat on the step and watched the sky darken above the gray-leaved Russian olive tree that grew in the center of the yard. The barn swallows emerged to dip and dive for insects.

She asked the question that had been nagging in the back of her mind since she'd run out to keep him from driving off. "Did you feel like I pushed you into staying for dinner?"

He gave her a look and a shrug. "It's all right."

She wanted to shake him. "So you did, then? You really did want to get out of here." She turned away from him.

"Hey." Gently, he caught her chin. "I stayed. I'm here."

But only after she'd pressured him into it. *I'm pregnant,* she thought. *And I don't know how to tell you. I'm pregnant, and Tess just lost her baby....*

She caught his wrist and carefully pushed his hand away. "It hurt, that's all. To think you'd just leave like that."

"But I didn't...." His voice was so soft. Underneath, though, she could hear the note of impatience.

A coldness went through her. At that moment she felt as if she didn't really know him—as if she never had. She searched his shadowed face, willing him to understand. "It's only that life is...so fragile. Today I got a scary lesson in how easily it can be lost. All I wanted was to see you. And then you came and you were so...distant. All *you* wanted was to get the heck out."

"Starr..."

"That's it, isn't? What you wanted? To go?"

He looked at her, hard. And then, with a low oath, he braced his elbows on his open knees and stared down at the clean boots Daniel had brought for him. "Sometimes I think we've gone too far with this."

Her stomach went queasy. And that cold feeling intensified. "Gone too far? How?"

Now he looked straight ahead, out toward the olive tree and the slowly dimming sky. "I drove like a madman, out there to tell your dad what had happened. I told him and he took off and then I told Jobeth. And then...well, I know what you mean. About wanting to be with me. Because that's all I thought of while we finished up burning out that damn never-ending ditch—that I had to see you, that nothing would be all right until I could get to you."

She wasn't following. What was the problem, then? This sounded *good.* "So what's wrong with that?"

He still didn't look at her. "Finally, we had the ditch clear. We opened the headgate farther upstream and we loaded the tools in the pickup. The hands hopped in back and Jobeth got in the cab with me. I started up the engine, threw up a rain of mud and grass as I peeled out of there. Jobeth said, 'Sheesh, Beau. Where's the fire?'" He made a low sound, shook his head. "Well, there was no fire. There was just…you. I wanted to get back to you. And that's pretty damn stupid, considering that in a couple of weeks, you're outta here. You won't be around to come back *to*."

The sky might be darkening to night, but to Starr, the world was suddenly suffused with a bold, shining light. She knew, then, how to tell him.

Of course. Before she spoke of the baby, she needed to make him see that she wouldn't leave him, after all—that she didn't *want* to leave. That she wanted, more than anything, to be right here for him to come home to, for the rest of their lives.

She put her hand on his arm, felt the corded power in it—and never wanted to let go. Slowly, he turned his head to look at her. He scanned her face, his mouth kind of twisted, as if just the sight of her caused him pain.

She had to make him see that she would never hurt him, that she would stay right here, beside him. That everything would be fine. "Oh, Beau. I've been thinking…."

"About what?" he asked, his tone not especially encouraging.

She blurted it out. "Beau, I really don't want to go. I could be happy here, at home, with you. I see that now."

He was already shaking his head. "That's crazy. You can't stay here. That wasn't the plan. We agreed—"

"So?" She cut him off in her urgency to make him see. "Who says we're not allowed to change our minds? Things happen. Things like you and me. Things like…love.''

He pulled his arm out from under her grip. Not a very good sign. But she wouldn't—couldn't—give up. ''Oh, listen. I can take that job Jerry's always offering me. And I can work freelance, too. And it doesn't matter, anyway. You know there's money, from my trust. I was thinking we could build ourselves a house of our own next to Daniel's, that we could…'' His hand came out, lightning fast and slid around the back of her neck. ''What?'' She blinked in surprise.

He hauled her face up to his and he kissed her, hard. She felt his teeth against her lips. He pulled away, then, as abruptly as he'd pressed his mouth to hers. ''No.''

''But—''

''We're keeping our agreement.'' He spoke low, his voice charged with a scary kind of intensity. His eyes burned into hers. ''You've got a whole damn life ahead of you. You're not changing everything because of me. No way I'm letting you give up your dreams for yourself, no way I'll spend your money to build a house so you can live where you don't want to be.''

''But that's just it. I *do* want to be here. And it's not like I'm a stranger to this kind of life. I've lived through a few Wyoming winters. My *family* is here. Whenever I'm away, I find myself longing for the next time I can get back.''

''No,'' he said, repeating the word with more insistence than before. He still had his hand around the back of her neck. He yanked her close again and pressed his forehead to hers. ''No,'' he said, as if he would drill the word into her mind. Then he let her go and started to stand.

She grabbed his arm again. "Wait. Please." He stayed seated beside her—but he didn't look happy about it. "Oh, why won't you believe me? I love you and I don't want to go."

"No," he said, more softly that time. "You're going to New York City, the way you planned." That part came out as a command.

Hurt and anger sizzled through her. She'd said she loved him and all he could say to that was no? And who did he think he was, to tell her that she *had* to go? She opened her mouth to tell him just what she thought of him giving her orders—then reconsidered. A shouting match wasn't going to get them anywhere.

She tried a different angle. "For a minute, let's forget about me and my big dreams, okay? What about you, Beau? I mean, you just said you couldn't wait to get home to me."

"That isn't the point."

"Yes, it is. It's exactly the point. You couldn't wait to get home to me. And I couldn't wait for you to be here. Can't you see? We both just want to be together. And there's no reason why we—"

"No."

She flinched as if it slapped her. "I just don't get it. What's the matter with you? Are you going to try and tell me you'll be glad when I'm gone?"

"I never said that."

"Then why won't you just—"

"Stop."

"But I—"

"We agreed how it would be. That's not gonna change."

"Why not? Why *can't* things change? Look at me, look at the person I am now. I'm not the girl you knew six years ago. And you, Beau. You've made a whole new life for yourself."

"Yeah. A new life. A new life on my own."

"That's right. So take a big chance. Make a life with me."

"You're not listening."

"Because you're not making sense."

"Oh, I'm making sense all right. It's damn simple. I'm never getting married, Starr. That much isn't ever going to change. I'd be no good at it—and you deserve better than an ex-con from a family of murdering crooks."

"But…" She ran out of steam. This wasn't going anywhere. And she could see by the set of his jaw that no matter what she said, she wasn't changing his mind tonight.

The way he was looking at her now, she wouldn't be changing his mind *ever*.

God. She had told him flat out that she loved him. And for that she'd got nothing but a command that she leave him.

"Starr…" His voice was softer now. He touched her shoulder.

She turned her head away, shoved at his placating hand. "Don't."

"C'mon. Look at me."

She didn't look at him. She couldn't. She stared off past the last post at the end of the porch, toward the fence at the side of the yard, and beyond that, to the pastureland rolling out under the reddening sky dotted here and there with grazing cattle. One of Tess's roosters crowed, long and lost-sounding, out behind the house, and a gust of sudden wind blew down the porch, stirring her hair, so she had to swipe a few wild strands away from her eyes.

"Starr…"

In the end, she couldn't resist him. Damn her for a fool, she never could. She met his waiting gaze. "What?"

There was pain in his eyes, a lonely kind of hurt. "You gotta know, you're the only woman in my mind. You always have been, since that first day I saw you…" He gestured toward the driveway that curved around to the barn and the sheds. "Wearing that short, tight black skirt and that T-shirt with no bra under it, strutting across the yard that hot summer day you came here to stay. But how I feel about you—and what I'm capable of doing. They're not the same. I'm just…I'm not doing that, Starr. Not ever."

She didn't understand—didn't *want* to understand. "Not doing what?"

"You know what. Marriage. Kids. That whole family thing. It's not for me. I thought you knew that. I told you that, six years ago. I'm never getting married and I'm sure as hell never going to mess up some poor kid's life by trying to be a dad."

She couldn't be hearing this. "But…that was then. Everything's different now."

"For you, maybe. Me, I'm still a Tisdale. The first honest Tisdale, in two generations, I like to think. Maybe I'll never be able to vote in the state of Wyoming, now I'm an ex-con. Maybe in a lot of ways,

I'll always be a second-class citizen. I'm okay with that. I've got honest work to do and Daniel to look after. I'm…contented with that. Good with it, you know?''

"Well then, why not take the next step? Why not—"

"Listen. Try to hear what I'm saying. As far as the marriage and family thing goes, where I grew up, it meant shouting and hitting and burning and cutting.''

"But…that's crazy. You and me, we'd never be like that.''

"It doesn't matter.''

"Of course it matters, it matters more than anything. *Love* matters. You and me and what we have, what we can be, together. That's everything. That's… what life's about.''

"I know that.''

"Well, then, if you know it, I don't see why you can't—"

"Damn it, Starr. Yeah. I know it. I know it up here.'' He tapped his forehead. "But in here.'' He touched his chest. "In the place I live and breathe, in my guts and in my heart.'' He was shaking his head. "Here, I only know that having a wife and a family is a recipe for disaster. It's not for me.''

She gaped at him. "That's ridiculous. You're not your dad or your awful brothers. You're a good man. You've made a decent life for yourself. You've got a right to—"

"It's not what I want. I'm just not cut out for it.''

"How can you say that?''

"Because it's the truth.'' He got up—and that time

she didn't try to stop him. "Look. I think it's about time Daniel and me got going."

She stared up at him looming above her. In his face, she could see clearly his eagerness to be gone.

Though inside she was reeling from all the awful things he'd said, she considered trying to stop him....

But if she kept him here, kept at him, she would start shouting. She'd call him some ugly things and she'd do it really loud. The hands in the trailers across the yard would hear her. Worse than that, her little brother and her fourteen-year-old sister would hear, too. The last thing Ethan and Jo needed—especially after a day like today—was to hear their big sister screaming at Beau.

"Yeah," she said tightly. "You're right. You'd better just go."

Chapter Eleven

Tess came home on Tuesday, with circles under her eyes and a determined smile on her face. Zach carried her upstairs to bed. She stayed there for about two hours, and then she came down to the kitchen and sat at the table and warned Edna not to put too many onions in the Swiss steak.

"I've been cutting back on them," grumbled Edna. Starr, at the sink as usual, wielding her trusty potato peeler, tried not to roll her eyes. Edna was always cutting back on the onions—and yet her gravy inevitably came out thick and pungent with them. "And you should be upstairs in bed where Zach put you," Edna scolded.

"It's too quiet up there—Ethan!"

Ethan came flying in from the great room. "Yeah, Mom?" Lately, it took him forever to come when you called him. But not this time.

"How 'bout a story?"

His eyes lit up. "Right now—when it's not even bedtime?"

"Right now."

He went and got a stack of Dr. Seuss books and scrambled up on her lap, even though for weeks now, he'd been telling everyone that he was too big for sitting on laps anymore. Tess read him the familiar stories. From the corner of her eye, Starr saw how Tess fondly stroked his hair and twice pressed a kiss to his temple. He allowed these attentions, though as a rule in recent weeks he would squirm away from open displays of affection.

Once, Tess looked up when Starr glanced her way. Their gazes locked. A soft smile curved Tess's mouth—and the sadness in her eyes was fathoms deep.

Edna fed the hands early and the family ate in the dining room. Starr watched the tender looks that passed between her father and his wife. They were so lucky, to have each other at a time like this.

Starr remembered when they'd first gotten married—that year she came back to live on the Rising Sun. Even a mixed-up sixteen-year-old could see they had problems. Then, they'd slept in separate rooms…

But they'd worked it out. They'd built a good life together, found a strong, abiding love. The kind of love that would see them through this awful loss. They were a living, breathing example of what a marriage could be.

They had what Beau seemed to think just wasn't possible.

Later, Ethan watched a few cartoons and Zach sat

in the easy chair he'd reclaimed from his son and read for a while. The women played Scrabble.

Edna went back to her place at ten. Starr stayed downstairs after everyone else went up. She watched a movie—a romance, where the girl got the guy and everyone was happy at the end.

It was late when the movie ended. She turned off the lights and went upstairs to her old bedroom.

The next night, Wednesday, after the dishes were cleaned up, Starr decided to get a head start on some articles she'd said she'd put together for the following week's *Clarion*. She was typing away when Tess spoke from the open doorway.

"Working hard, I see."

It was the oddest moment. Tess stood in exactly the same place she'd stood Saturday afternoon, when she came to tell Starr that something was wrong. Now, except for those fading shadows under her eyes and a certain sad reserve in her manner, she looked well.

Tough things happened. You got over it. Life went on.

Starr spun her swivel chair to face her stepmother. "Just getting a little ahead for a change." Tess gave her a hopeful smile. Starr knew she was waiting for an invitation. "Come on in. Shut the door."

Tess pushed the door closed and sat on the bed. "I haven't seen Beau around...."

Starr had been expecting that one. "Me neither." After their little talk on the porch Saturday night, he'd been conspicuously absent. Which was fine with Starr—or so she kept trying to tell herself.

"Your dad says you've been staying here at the house since Saturday."

She'd been needed here—at least, at first. But now, with Edna back to help run the house and cook the meals and Tess home safe and on her feet, the excuse was starting to wear a little thin. "Yeah. Guess I'll go on back to the cabin tonight, soon as I finish up on the computer."

"I didn't mean to get you thinking that you *have* to go. We love having you here, close, with us."

Starr wrinkled up her nose. "You always say just the right thing."

"It's only the truth. I'd like nothing better than if you stayed."

"It's time I went back." Her own place *was* important to her—whether Beau was in it or not.

Tess sighed. "That's your choice, of course." She smoothed the blue-and-purple bedspread with a light hand. "I've been meaning to tell you how grateful I am that you were here Saturday." She smiled, a wistful kind of smile. "I squeezed your poor fingers so hard… Didn't break any bones, did I?"

Starr held up her hand and wiggled the fingers. "Nope. Still works just fine. And I'm glad I was here, too—though I did feel pretty helpless."

"Helpless…" Tess seemed to ponder the word. "I know what you mean." She smoothed the bedspread some more. "I'm going to be all right, you know. Eventually."

"Yeah. I know you will."

"But what about you?"

Starr's throat clutched—just a little. Tess did amaze her. Even at a time like this, when Tess ought to be concentrating on her own loss, she took the time to find out what was bothering Starr. "I'm okay. Really…"

Tess looked at her for a long, measuring moment. "Don't want to talk about it, huh?"

"You don't need to hear it."

"But I *want* to hear it—as soon as you're ready to share with me." Tess stood. "And now, I guess I'd better let you work."

"Tess?"

"Umm?"

"Thanks."

"I'm here. A little the worse for wear, maybe. A little—" she seemed to seek the right word, and settled on "—brokenhearted. But I'm here. Any time. Never forget that."

Starr returned to the cabin later that night. She took a long bath, thinking the soothing water would relax her, make it easier to sleep.

The bath didn't work. She lay there alone in that bed for an hour or so, then she got up and pulled on her robe and went out to the front step.

She was sitting there watching the stars, wondering if she was ever going to get to sleep, when the twin beams of headlights cut the night. The two lights bounced along over the ruts in the twisting dirt driveway—headed for her place.

Beau.

Starr resisted opposing urges: to leap up and run out to meet him, and to slip inside, turn off the light, latch the door and not open it no matter how hard he pounded on it. She didn't want to see his face, she told herself—at the same time as her foolish heart beat faster with longing the closer that pickup came.

What was there to say to him? She'd pretty much said it all—well, except for the part about the baby.

And yeah, okay. The one point she hadn't made was the main one. But she wasn't blaming herself too much for not saying it. He'd told her he was never going to be anybody's dad, for Pete's sake. Chirping up with "Well, too bad, you're *gonna* be one..."

Uh-uh.

The pickup pulled in next to the Suburban. The engine went quiet and the headlights blinked out, leaving the night seeming darker than before. For several long seconds, he just sat there, a shadow behind the wheel. Maybe he regretted deciding to come.

She could relate to that. A part of her wouldn't have minded in the least if he'd just stayed away, left her alone to take her wounded heart and her unborn baby and get on that plane for New York, after all.

She rose to her feet as he opened his door. He came around the front of the vehicle and strode toward her, halting an arm's distance away.

"Well," she said, staring up into his shadowed face, her heart knocking hard against her ribs—but her tone as cool as the wind that ruffled her hair. "What a surprise. I was beginning to think I'd seen the last of you."

He reached for her. She tried to jerk back, to escape his hands, but he caught her anyway and pulled her into him.

Outraged, she commanded, "Let me go." He held on, leaving her to squirm and struggle in his hold, furious at him for daring to grab her when she didn't want to be held—and also, somewhere deep inside, rejoicing at his nearness, at the feel of his body against hers.

"Starr," he said, and that got to her—her name on his lips. She let him hold her, pressing spread hands against his chest to keep him from daring any additional intimacies.

He wanted to kiss her—she could see it in his eyes, in the hungry way his gaze kept tracking to her mouth. He wanted to kiss her and sweep her up and carry her inside, take her to bed where they could do the one thing they both agreed on.

"Damn it, I missed you," he whispered. His heart pounded too fast under her hand.

She breathed in the scent of him, hungry for him as he was for her—and fighting that hunger with every ounce of will and self-respect she possessed. She schooled her voice to an even tone. "I've been right here the whole time."

He glared down at her. "Waiting for me to change my mind?"

Fresh anger blazed through her. "No way. I got the point. Your mind is made up and I'd better get used to it—which has me kind of wondering what you're doing here."

"I... Damn it." He let her go so abruptly she almost stumbled. "You're right." He turned on his heel.

She knew she should just let him leave. But some contrary part of her had to have the last word. "Beau." He kept on walking. "Wait." He stopped and faced her again. "Why did you come here?"

He looked her up and down, that blue gaze burning

everywhere it touched. "I told you. It was killin' me. I had to see you...."

She hitched up her chin. "So here I am. What now?"

He swore. "Okay, you got me. I'm a jackass for showing up here."

He'd get no argument on that one. "Yeah. You are."

He looked down at his boots, shook his head. "I'm sorry, Starr."

Tears pushed at the back of her throat and she had to bite her lip to keep it from trembling. "Sorry just doesn't cut it."

His head came up. His eyes were hard, his face set against her—against any hope that they might find their way to a shared life together. "Look. It's how it is. I can't be what you want me to be and I'm not going to lie about it."

She laughed then. Laughed, to keep those pointless tears from falling. "There's a great line from an old movie... '*Can't* lives on *won't* street.' That's pretty much you, Beau, don't you think?"

"You just don't get it." He spoke through clenched teeth. "You don't *want* to get it."

"Well, yeah. That's the truth. I don't want to get that I'm the only woman who matters to you, that you've never forgotten me after all these years, that you can't stay away from me, can't keep your hands off me...but still, at the end of the summer, you're sending me to New York—whether I want to leave you or not. I don't get how, if you can't stay away from me now, you're going to stand it when I'm gone for good."

"Damn it, we had an agreement."

"Don't start in with that again. I heard it all before."

"What the hell do you want me to say?"

"Nothing—not if all you're gonna do is tell me what I already know."

They stared at each other, the short distance between them a yawning chasm of a thousand miles.

"I'm gone, then," he said at last. "I won't come back."

"Well, all right, then. Goodbye."

She didn't stick around to watch him leave. Whirling, she raced up the steps and into the cabin, shutting the door against the sound of his pickup starting up and driving off.

The damn, useless tears tried to rise again. She rested her forehead against the rough wood of the door, sniffing like crazy to keep them at bay.

But they wouldn't be held back. In the end, she let them take her, let the great, gulping sobs roll through her. She slid down the door and sat there on the floor, shoulders shaking, the tears streaming free down her cheeks, crying for the love, the marriage—the family—that was never going to be.

Chapter Twelve

Thursday, Friday, Saturday, Sunday, Monday...

The days crept by. Starr went to work and helped out at the main house and fought the growing awareness that she couldn't keep hiding from the thing she hadn't said.

By the Tuesday after their confrontation on the cabin steps, with only six days left until she was scheduled to leave for New York, Starr knew she was going to have to put aside her broken heart and swallow her wounded pride and find a way to tell Beau that whether he wanted kids or not, he was going to be a dad.

In the cabin, long after she should have been in bed, she sat at the table under the hard light of the bulb that hung from a bare beam overhead and tried to decide how to give him the big news.

A phone call?

"Hi, Beau. By the way, I forgot to mention it the other night when I told you never to come near me again, but I'm having your baby. Just thought you should know…"

Yuck. Starr put her head in her hands. "Yuck, yuck, yuck…" She raked her hair back out of her eyes and sat up tall again.

No. Not a phone call. No matter how personally fed up a woman might be with a man, when she laid news like this on him, she pretty much had a duty to say it to his face.

But *what* to say?

"Simple," she muttered. "Direct." She had to just…get it out there. Bite the bullet. Say the words. "Beau," she said to the rough plank walls of the cabin. "Beau, I'm pregnant.…"

Oh, God. She hung her head again. There had to be a more graceful way to do it. Some way to kind of ease into it…

Yeah. There had to be at least fifty ways to tell a man you were having his baby.

Too bad she could only come up with one: *Beau, I'm pregnant.…*

Starr threw back her head and groaned at that bare, glaring light bulb overhead.

Tomorrow, she vowed, blinking away the afterimages caused by the brightness. She would do it tomorrow—get it over with, somehow.

Gently, but firmly: *Beau, I'm pregnant.*

And then she'd have done her duty. He could step up to the plate and try to be some sort of father—or she would manage without him.

* * *

In the early morning, before she went into town, Starr stopped at the main house and enlisted Tess's aid in baking a couple of blackberry pies.

"Pies can make a fine peace offering," Tess suggested hopefully as she rolled out the dough.

Starr only grunted and sugared the berries.

That evening, Starr packed up the pies and drove over to Daniel's.

Daniel answered her knock, a paper napkin hanging from the neck of his shirt. "Starr." His broad face lit up. "Where have you been lately?"

It was a good question. One she had no intention of answering. "Oh!" she chirped, faking lightheartedness for all she was worth. "I caught you at supper...."

"We're just finishing up."

She held up the pies stacked in their Tupperware containers and announced brightly, "Perfect timing then, huh?" Well, if there *was* such a thing in a case like this.

He beamed all the wider. "You do know the way straight to a man's heart." Sure, she did. As long as the heart wasn't Beau's. "Come on in."

I cannot do this, she thought as she stepped over the threshold and followed Daniel through the front room to the kitchen.

"Look who's here," Daniel announced when Beau looked up from the table.

It was not a good moment. His eyes met hers and narrowed. She could almost hear him thinking, *What the hell are you doing here?* And was the oven on? It seemed way too hot in there. "Hello, Starr."

She swallowed. "Hi, Beau. I, um, brought the dessert."

"Well," he said, "great." His tone communicated it was anything but. His gaze dropped—for an instant—to her mouth.

Never mind about the oven. The heat was inside her. It sizzled all through her—just from the way he was looking at her mouth.

She whirled away from him before she melted to a puddle of hopeless lust and longing right where she stood. *Get a grip,* she commanded herself. "I'll put the coffee on, why don't I?"

Daniel asked after Tess and gave a report on his own improving health as the coffee dripped. When the pot was finally full, Starr poured the men each a cup and cut them each a slice of pie.

Daniel frowned. "Aren't you having any?"

Her stomach was so knotted up, the thought of eating made her want to gag. Still, she gave the old sweetheart a blinding smile. "Well, sure I will."

She dished up a small piece and took an empty chair—directly across from Beau. He looked at her, a thousand questions in his eyes. She picked up her fork and concentrated on her plate. Even if she couldn't eat the pie, looking at it kept her from having to meet that brooding, too-watchful blue gaze.

Daniel had two slices and yakked away as he gobbled them down. She was so nerved up over the job ahead, she hardly heard what the older man was saying until he asked her if something was bothering her.

Blinking, she glanced up from her careful study of her untouched pie. "Uh, no. I'm fine."

Beau spoke up then. "You're not eating your pie."

To her, the words sounded like some sort of accusation.

She wanted to pick up that slice of pie and throw it right in his face. But she really had to watch her temper. If she had a fit every time something he said rubbed her the wrong way, their baby would be all grown up before she ever managed to tell him she was having one.

"Well, you know, the truth is, I had a big dinner." A flat-out lie. But only a little one. She pushed her plate away. Now or never, as they say. "Beau. I wonder if we could take a little stroll?"

"Good idea," said Daniel before Beau bothered to answer. He tipped his balding head Beau's way. "Be nice to him, now. He's had a—"

"Daniel," Beau cut him off.

"Ah," said Daniel. "Forgive an old man." He winked at Starr. "Talking out of turn. Gotta watch that."

Beau pushed back his chair. "Let's go, then."

She followed him out. When they got down the front steps, she caught up with him and they strolled, side by side but careful not to touch, across the yard, out to that little stream north of the house.

They stood on the bank under a wind-stirred cottonwood, not far from the place they'd sat that day she first came to him, when he said they could see each other—if she'd give it a week's thought first.

She stared out over the water and tried not to remember the happiness and promise she'd felt on that other day. How long ago was that—six, seven weeks? It seemed longer. It seemed years away....

She sent him a glance.

Those watchful eyes were waiting. "You shocked the hell out of me, showing up here."

Irritation prickled through her. She ordered herself to ignore it. She simply had to get past getting mad at him for everything he said. Really, if she tried a little harder to be fair, she'd have to admit that his tone hadn't been critical—just wary. Just…not getting it.

And why should he get it? She'd told him to stay away—and now here she was, showing up at his door, leading him out to walk by the creek.

"I'm sorry," she said.

A smile kind of tugged at the corner of his mouth. "Sorry doesn't cut it." They were her own words of the other night, given back to her. With considerably better humor, she had to admit.

"Good point," she admitted with a sigh.

"So…something going on?"

And there it was. The moment to say it: *Beau, I'm pregnant.* "Well, I just…"

"Yeah?"

She just…couldn't quite do it. "Uh, let's sit down." With that easy long-boned male grace that always stole her breath, he dropped to the bank. She sat down beside him. "I…"

"Yeah?"

She cleared her throat. "Um…" Her mind went skittering away from the words. Instead of saying them, she asked, "What was that about, with Daniel?"

He studied her face for a long, too-quiet moment. Then he shrugged. "I got a call today, from a certain lawyer down in Rawlins.…"

A call from a lawyer… "T.J.?" His rotten oldest

brother had been in prison so long, sometimes it seemed like he'd never been out.

Beau nodded. "He lost another appeal." His mouth quirked in a wry smile. "Too bad for T.J.—but a good thing for every honest, upstanding citizen in the state of Wyoming."

"So what happens now?"

He was shaking his head. "Forget T.J. for a minute. What are you doing here? I don't get it. The other night you sent me away. I didn't like it, but I gotta admit, I understood. Now, here you are, bringing on the berry pies, asking me to take a little walk with you. It's pretty damn confusing, Starr."

He was so right.

And she could not do it. She couldn't tell him. Not today…

"Starr?"

"I just…well, now I've had some time to think about it, I guess I'm realizing it's not very fair for me to, um, expect things of you that you warned me from the first weren't going to be happening." Surprisingly, as she fumbled over the words, she found there was actually some truth in them. "I keep thinking about six years ago, how it ended so ugly. I keep thinking how important you are, in my life, even if you won't be, um, everything I wish you could be. I keep thinking that I'd like to do a better job of it, of you and me, this time. That I'd like to leave here a week from now with some kind of…oh, I don't know. Some kind of peace and understanding between us."

"You think that's possible?" His voice was low. There was hope in it now—and the darkness of doubt, as well.

"Well, I'd sure like to give it a try." *Yes,* she was thinking, warmth spreading through her. She really did want peace between them. Though he couldn't give her the love she longed for, he *had* given her a baby. They were going to have to deal with that. If they couldn't be a family, they should at least manage somehow to put the anger and hurt behind them.

She thought of Tess then, of the sadness in her eyes, of her brave smiles. Tess had lost her baby. But she would get on with her life. She would cherish what she did have: her husband, her children, the good life they had made. Tess was the kind of woman Starr longed to be.

So okay. Starr had lost something important, too— what might have been with Beau. But you couldn't live your life looking back on might-have-beens. You had to take what you still had, make it work the best you could.

"We've got a few days left," she said, accepting within herself that she would be on that plane to New York, after all, as she'd originally planned. "Why can't we make the most of them?"

He was frowning. "Go back…the way we were?"

She almost said yes, but then she considered all that would mean. Maybe not. "I don't know. Maybe that's not possible. And maybe it's not a good idea, anyway. The truth is, when you touch me, when you make love to me, I can't help hoping for things that aren't going to happen."

He asked, sounding cautious, "Hands off, you mean?"

It was exactly what she meant. She wanted to come to some kind of peace with him before she left. She didn't think she could do that if they kept stirring up the flames. "Yeah," she confessed. "That's pretty much what I was thinking. Is that…something you could do?"

He grunted. "Maybe. If I stayed drunk all the time."

"No. I don't think that would…" She saw the gleam in his eyes. "Ha ha. Very funny."

He caught her hand. The familiar thrill shimmered through her as he pressed a kiss to the back of it.

She dared to ask, "Should I take that as a yes, then? We can have our last few days, in a hands-off kind of way?"

With clear reluctance, he let go of her fingers. "You're a hell of a woman, Starr."

"Does that mean yes—or no?"

"It means you knock me over. You blow me away. You always have."

"Yes or no?"

He answered at last. "What you said—about not wanting it to end ugly like it did before, about us doing a better job this time of…letting each other go?"

Letting each other go. It sounded so sad. Still, she did feel hopeful. "Yeah?"

"I feel the same way."

She gulped. "So…"

"So yeah, Starr. I want us to be okay with each other. If there's some way I can keep you from hating me when you go, I'll take it. I'll take these last few days with you—and I'll keep my hands off you if that's how you want it."

Chapter Thirteen

For the first time in over a week, Starr actually felt good about something. Okay, she hadn't managed to lay the big news on him yet. But she would get to that. She would.

She had five days—well, four, since she knew she wouldn't do it tonight. And now they were speaking again, now they were on friendly terms, it should be a lot easier. She'd find the right moment.

Eventually…

"I'm glad—that we're going to give ourselves another chance to do this right." It kind of shocked her that she actually meant it.

He nodded. "So am I."

"So." She gathered up her knees and rested her cheek on them. "What about T.J.? What happens to him now?"

Beau picked up a pebble from the yellowing grass. "Well, I don't think he's got his date with the needle yet."

She touched his arm with a tentative hand. "More appeals, you mean?"

He looked down at where she touched him, then into her eyes. She saw the warning there: If it's hands off, then don't touch *me*. She pulled her hand away and he tossed the pebble into the stream. "Yeah. That's what the lawyer said." From the tree overhead, a jay scolded them. Beau looked at her again. "The lawyer asked me to go down there."

She studied his face. Unreadable. "T.J. wants to see you?"

He shifted, stretching his long legs out, crossing them at the ankles. "Yeah. He asks to see me every now and then. God only knows why. I sure as hell don't want to see him."

"When will you go?"

He rested back on his elbows. "I didn't say I'd go."

"It doesn't matter if you said it or not, I know you will. Whatever awful things he did, T.J.'s still your brother."

That jay kept squawking. "Did you have to remind me?"

"When will you go?"

He uncrossed his legs. "Tomorrow morning. I can see my brother in the afternoon, visit the lawyer afterward and be home by eight or nine tomorrow night."

A long drive, up and back. Lots of time to talk. It could be the perfect opportunity to say what needed saying—plus, well, he shouldn't have to go down there alone. Someone should be there with him. Someone who cared for him....

"Is Daniel going with you?"

"He offered. But I'll do it alone."

"Why should you?"

"It's just better that way, I think."

"Better because...?"

He stared out across the narrow stream, toward the bank on the other side and the pasture beyond. "Hell. It's not going to be a happy kind of trip. No reason I've got to drag Daniel along. Plus, he's doing a lot better now. There's plenty of work to do around here and he can keep after it. Just because I'm wasting a whole day on a trip I don't want to make doesn't mean he has to waste the day, too."

"Would you...take me?"

He looked straight at her. "Bad idea."

"No. Really. I want to go."

He moved away an inch or two. "You can't go in with me. Only family allowed in there—not that you'd want to go in."

"I can wait in the car."

"Starr. There's no damn point."

"Yeah, there is. It's a long drive. You can use a little company on the way." She slid over a fraction, closing the gap he had made between them. Her arm brushed his—but only once. She was careful not to let it happen again. "I promise to keep up a steady stream of meaningless chatter." *Except for the part about the baby,* she silently amended, *if the moment seems right and I can get up the nerve...*

He looked at her then. *Really* looked at her. In his eyes, she saw his reluctance to make the trip, saw the knowledge that he had to—saw that he wouldn't mind at all having company on the way. "You'd be bored to death."

"I'll bring a good book."

"You have to work."

"Jerry's a flexible boss. It's one of his best things." She reached out—and again had to remind herself of the terms she'd just laid down. She let her hand drop to the grass. "Come on. Sometimes you have to do things you wish you didn't. But there's no law that says you've got to do them alone."

He came to pick her up at daybreak, looking grim. The first thing he said when she opened the door to him was, "You know you don't have to do this."

She waved his objections away and suggested they take the Suburban. "Roomier," she said with a cheerful smile. "And the ride is smoother. And I'll even let you drive."

He grumbled, but they did it her way. They rolled out of the yard as the sky bled to orange off toward town.

It was a much quieter ride than she'd intended. He really didn't want to talk. She'd ask a question and he'd answer with a "Yeah," or "Uh-uh" or a low grunt that could have meant just about anything.

Eventually she gave up on making casual conversation. They sped down the highway, the land getting flatter and drier as they went. Her idea that she might tell him about the baby seemed ridiculous now.

It was so not the time.

Still, she didn't regret coming along. Once or twice he looked over at her, just a quick glance. She would smile at him and he'd turn his attention back to the road ahead.

"Thank you," he said once, so low she almost didn't hear the words.

"Anytime," she replied, thinking that whether she told him today or not, it didn't really matter. It was the right thing to come with him, the right thing to be there, at his side, for this.

And besides, she wasn't completely giving up on telling him today. Maybe, if it felt right, she'd do it on the way home....

He wouldn't let her go out to the South Facility with him. He said she didn't need to be anywhere near that place. He let her off in town, at a coffee shop on Cedar Street. She could eat and read the book she'd brought—maybe look around town a little, check out the shops and the Territorial Prison, which had been shut down years ago and now was a big tourist attraction.

She had a phone with her. He said he'd call before he started the short trip back to town. They could go to the lawyer's office together.

It was after four when he returned. She sat at the counter in the coffee shop, nursing a Sprite, her book open and ignored in front of her, watching out the wide bank of windows as clouds gathered in the sky, turning it leaden gray with a promise of rain for the trip home. He pushed through the glass doors, spotted her and gestured with a toss of his head.

She'd already set her money down. She grabbed her book, thanked the waitress and hurried out to meet him.

"Come on, let's go," was all he said, his face set. Determined. Closed off to any questions.

They got back in the Suburban and drove the few blocks to a flat-roofed office building on Pine Street.

Taft Eldridge and Associates, Attorneys at Law, was on the second floor: a cramped cubicle that smelled of mildew. Battered file cabinets huddled together on one wall. There was a grimy window with a ledge crowded with scraggly-looking potted plants. By the time they got there, the rain had started. Fat drops blew against the dirty glass and slithered down.

The attorney rose from behind a desk piled high with precariously stacked manila folders. He wore a wrinkled white dress shirt, sleeves rolled to the elbows and a pair of equally rumpled gray slacks. His tie hung loose around his neck.

"Come in, come in. Have a seat."

Starr and Beau sandwiched themselves into a pair of orange plastic chairs between the desk and the looming file cabinets.

"Taft Eldridge," the lawyer said. "Mr. Tisdale, right?" He extended his hand.

Beau reached across the piles of folders and they shook. "I'm T.J.'s brother, Beau."

"Ahem. Yes. Let's see now…" The lawyer sat again and began rummaging through the folders. A pile of them started to tip. He caught it before the whole stack slid from the desk and whipped out a folder from near the middle. "Tisdale…ah. Here…" He looked at Beau. "Mr. Tisdale, though I have informed your brother that we've not yet exhausted our options in his case, he wishes that you, as his next-of-kin, should take possession of his personal belongings at this point.'' He set the folder to the side, pulled out a drawer and withdrew a large yellow envelope, lumpy with whatever was inside. "I'll need identification— just as a matter of form.''

Beside her, Beau sat very still, looking straight ahead, his face a bleak mask.

"Ahem. Mr. Tisdale…''

Beau made a low sound of disgust. "You got me in here for *this?* I don't need that junk.''

"Ahem. Well. It is your brother's wish—''

"You think I give a damn what T.J. wishes?''

The lawyer sat back in his chair. "Mr. Tisdale, if you don't choose to accept these items, that is, of course, your right.''

"Well, Mr. Eldridge.'' Beau's voice was heavy on the sarcasm. "Thank you for telling me.''

Starr was keeping her mouth shut—with effort. But when Beau glanced her way, she couldn't help giving him a questioning look. What was the big deal? Why couldn't he just take the envelope, if it was something his brother wanted him to have?

Beau gave her a hot glare—and then waved a hand. "All right, fine. Whatever.'' He took out his wallet and showed the lawyer his driver's license.

"Ah,'' said the lawyer with a sour little smile. "Good. I see we're all in order.'' He stood again, long enough to grab the stack of folders directly in front of Beau. When he couldn't find another spot on the desk, he plunked the pile on the floor beside his chair. "Now then.'' He took a paper from T.J.'s folder and set the paper down in the space he'd cleared in front of Beau. "Sign on the line. It says you've claimed the envelope containing the contents of your brother's pockets at the time of his arrest.''

Beau took the pen the lawyer offered and scrawled his name.

''Here you go, then.'' Taft Eldridge handed Beau the envelope. ''You two folks have a real nice day.''

When they got out to the street, the rain was coming down hard. They made a break for the Suburban, jumping in and hauling the doors shut as fast as they could against the downpour. Beau threw the unopened envelope behind the seat. Starr longed to ask him to open it right then. But the look on his face warned her not to go there. She hooked up her seat belt.

He started the engine, gunning it. She sent him a warning glance—but kept her mouth shut. With the windshield wipers slapping at the rain, they set off.

He drove too fast, sliding around a corner, with the tires screeching in protest. He raced through a yellow light, barely getting out of the intersection before it went to red. She gripped the armrest and kept quiet— until the next light, where he came within an inch of rear-ending a blue van.

''Beau. I'm not liking this. You'd better slow down.''

He sent her a lowering look and swore beneath his breath—but he did take it a little easier. Or at least he did until they got out of town onto the two-lane highway that wound its way to Casper. By then, as the rain beat down, making a blur of the road, Beau was once again driving too fast.

Twice, she asked him to slow it down. Both times, he did, but then, after a few minutes, he'd pick up speed again. They rode in a thick silence to the sound of the wipers beating at the rain.

The encounter with his brother had really gotten to him. That was obvious. But was it necessary to get in a wreck over it?

"Pull over," she finally commanded, when they were maybe twenty miles out of Rawlins and the speedometer hovered at seventy—way too fast for the treacherous conditions and the narrow, winding road. "Pull over now and let me drive."

He let his foot off the gas and they slowed to forty. "Happy?"

"Not particularly—since experience tells me you'll only speed up again. I mean it, Beau. Just pull over."

Finally, he did as she asked, easing the big vehicle onto the shoulder. He leaned on his door and got out without saying a word. A few seconds later, he appeared at her side door. She clambered over the console. Water dripping off his hat—and the rest of him for that matter—he took the seat she'd vacated. "Happy now?" he grumbled, giving the door a good slam.

She decided against dignifying that one with an answer. Hitching up her seat belt, she put the Suburban in gear and carefully eased out onto the streaming asphalt.

They rode along in a loaded silence for a while, Starr straining to make out the broken white line in the center of the road, telling herself to be glad that at least there was hardly any traffic. If she did wander over that line she could barely see, there was a good chance she wouldn't hit anything before she got herself back to the right side of the road.

The silence from Beau's side of the car only seemed to get thicker. Gloomier.

She'd been driving for about ten minutes when she dared to send him a look and to tartly suggest, "You know, it's not my fault that your brother's a—"

"Look out!"

She snapped her gaze back to the road in time to see the deer leaping out in front of them. Stomping the brake, she swerved to miss it—and she did.

The deer got away clean.

They weren't so lucky. The tires hydroplaned. They went skidding along the edge of the road as she tried to get the wheel back under control.

She didn't succeed. They hit the ditch beyond the shoulder, only stopping with a crunching crash when the Suburban drove itself into the bank on the far side.

Chapter Fourteen

The Suburban revved high and hard—and then died. The wipers beat on, fighting back the driving rain. Starr put up both hands to shove the already-deflating air bag out of her way.

Beau shoved at his own air bag. "You okay?"

"Yeah. Considering."

He unhooked his seat belt and pushed open his door. Water flowed in. He hauled it shut. "Great. We'd better get out of here. No telling how fast the ditch will fill up." He shoved at his air bag some more, so he could see out over the hood. "Hood looks a little crumpled. But the engine sounded okay when it died. Maybe we can..." He didn't finish. They were both looking out the back windshield. They were wedged in good. The Suburban was going nowhere without the help of a tow truck and a nice, big winch. Beau took the keys from the ignition. The windshield wipers stopped in midswipe.

Except for the driving beat of the rain and the occasional creaking sound from the crunched up Suburban, it was quiet. Starr shook her head. He'd been driving like a maniac—and *she'd* ended up getting them in a wreck.

"Hey." He squeezed her shoulder. She'd never been so grateful for a reassuring touch, hands-off rule be damned. "Not your fault," he said. "We're lucky you were driving. Going nice and slow…" At least the humor was back in his eyes. Too bad it took a wreck to put it there. "Okay?" he asked. When she nodded, he reached over the seat and grabbed her purse.

"Take the envelope, too."

He sent her an irritated glance. "Why? It's only paper. The damn thing'll disintegrate in this downpour."

"Give it to me." He didn't look thrilled about it, but he did as she asked. She folded it and managed to stuff it in her purse—where she found her cell phone. "Shouldn't I call for a tow truck before we—?"

"What good's it gonna do? We can't wait out there in the pouring rain for the hours it'll probably take one to show up. We'll have to grab the first ride we can flag down and worry about the car when we get someplace safe and dry." It made sense, she supposed. "You got any flares?"

"Will a flare work—in this?"

"Sweetheart, a flare will work under water."

In spite of their predicament, her heart warmed at

the easy endearment. "In the emergency kit in the back…"

"I'll grab 'em on the way out. Let's go." He leaned on his door again. This time the water came pouring in. He swung his feet over into the ditch.

With a sigh of resignation, Starr hooked her purse over her shoulder and pushed open her own door.

When she stood up in the ditch, the swirling water came just below her knees. Lovely. Standing in it and standing *under* it, she was wet to the skin in seconds. She held on to the Suburban to keep the current from dragging her off her feet and made for the roadside bank, which was gooey and slick with mud. Sliding and slipping, she scrambled up to the side of the road.

Beau got to the shoulder a little ahead of her, even after a stop at the back-seat door. He held down a hand and hauled her up the rest of the way.

He had four flares. He gave her two. They went in opposite directions, setting them off at intervals, meeting in the middle by the ditched Suburban once the flares were lit.

"How're you holdin' up?"

The wind drove the rain against her face and she told herself to be glad that at least it wasn't hail—yet. "I've been better." She hunched her shoulders and looked down at her wet feet. "Wish I'd worn a sturdy pair of waterproof boots instead of sandals—but the good news is the rain washed most of the mud from between my toes."

He wrapped his arm around her, sharing his warmth and turning her so his body took most of the wind. It wasn't *that* cold—low sixties, maybe—but she was shivering as the rain beat down on them.

Within minutes, they spotted the headlights, twin dots of golden light coming their way. Beau waved both hands and shouted and Starr did the same.

An ancient Cadillac emerged from the downpour and sailed to a stop right beside them. The window slid down. A grizzled old guy in ratty suspenders, a dead cigar clamped between his yellowed teeth, leaned across the wide front seat. "A real toad-strangler, ain't it?" He pointed over his shoulder. "Get on in."

The window went up as Beau opened the rear door. Starr slid across the seat and Beau got in behind her.

"Oh, thank you," Starr said to the old guy in front.

"It ain't no problem." He popped the trunk latch. "Got some towels in the back…"

"We'll get 'em," Beau said. He grabbed Starr's hand. "Come on…"

She didn't see any reason they both needed to go back out there—but then she met his eyes. After the things he'd seen in his life, he wasn't getting out of that car and leaving her in it with a stranger behind the wheel.

The old man grumbled, "I'm not drivin' off without you, son." Then he lifted one suspendered shoulder in a shrug. "But a man's gotta do what a man's gotta do. If you feel you have to drag that poor girl out in that mess out there, do it fast and get it over with— look in the corner on the right side, under that pile of *Playboy* magazines…"

So Starr slid back across the seat and they emerged into the driving rain all over again. Beau led her back to the trunk and lifted it.

"Sheesh," she said, shivering, wrapping her arms around herself. That trunk was packed full of all kinds of stuff: a bicycle tire, an old computer monitor, piles of clothing, photo albums....

Beau didn't give her much time to check out the rest. He found the pile of *Playboy*s, shoved it over, grabbed the towels underneath and slammed the trunk. The old car bobbed like a yacht on a swell.

They hurried back to the rear door and got in the car again. Beau handed her a thick maroon towel monogrammed with an *F*.

The old guy turned around in his seat and winked at Starr. "I buy those *Playboy*s for the articles."

"Oh, of course..."

"Been a widower for over thirty years." He heaved a huge, blustery sigh. "Never looked at another woman since—well, except in pictures, acourse. Ah, Bathsheba. Empress of my heart. No one could ever come close to takin' her place, so why even try?" He indicated the towel she was using on her hair. "Those towels are my daughter, Delilah's. She probably knows I took 'em by now." He chortled to himself as if at some delicious private joke. "But a few towels'll be the least of the reasons she'll be mad at me. She doesn't like it when I take off. Says I'm too old." He grunted. "You're never too old, that's what *I* say."

Starr grinned at him. How could she help it? So what if his trunk was a garage sale begging to happen? She liked the naughty twinkle in his beady dark eyes.

They exchanged introductions. "Jones," the old man said. "Oggie Jones and pleased to meet ya. Where you need to go?"

Beau wiped his neck with the towel. "Anywhere we can hook up with a tow."

"Well, I'm headin' into Evansville—got a little

business to transact. I can let you off in Casper. How's that?''

Beau sent Starr a questioning look. She shrugged. ''That'd be just fine,'' he told the old man.

They set off, Oggie Jones hunched behind the wheel, peering into the downpour, chattering away. He told them of his family and his home in the Sierra gold country. Before the irreplaceable Bathsheba had ''shed the mortal coil,'' she had given Oggie three sons and a daughter, Delilah. He had a fourth son, he said, but not by the exalted Bathsheba. He met Starr's eyes in the rearview mirror. ''I know what you're thinkin'—and I meant what I said before. I ain't never been untrue. It was before I met my beautiful Bathsheba that my Jack was conceived.''

''Good to know,'' said Starr, huddling close to Beau, taking shameless advantage of the break in her own hands-off rule.

''Kids.'' The old man cackled. ''They're born, they drive you crazy—and then they grow up and drive you crazy some more. But then again, what else you gonna do with your time and your money?'' He shifted his cigar to the other side of his mouth. ''Family is what the world's about and that is a plain fact.''

Yes! Starr was thinking. She even dared to lift her head from the comfy spot on Beau's shoulder to see if—just maybe—he was getting the point. For her effort, she got a so-what kind of shrug. Not exactly the response she'd hoped for

But she wasn't complaining. She was out of the rain and she had Beau's arm around her—and maybe she ought to start seeing about getting her car towed.

She got out her cell, but couldn't raise a dial tone. So she snuggled close to Beau again and listened to Oggie rattle on.

At eight that evening, about twenty miles out of Casper, the rain stopped. Starr checked her phone again and it was working that time. She called the Rising Sun and told Tess about their problem.

"I don't know if we'll make it home tonight," she added after she'd explained their situation. "But we're okay and we'll see you at least by tomorrow sometime."

"How will you get back?"

"A rental car, I guess. When we figure it out, we'll let you know. Right now, we have a ride." She caught Oggie's eye in the rearview mirror and gave him a grin. "We'll probably end up in Casper for the night."

Tess offered to come on down and get them. Starr almost accepted. But then she slid a glance at Beau. Hey. This could be her big opportunity. In a whole night alone with him, she'd surely find the right moment to deliver the big news.

"Thanks. We'll manage."

"Call me," Tess instructed. "Let me know where you are when you stop for the night."

"I will. Promise. Tell Daniel?"

"Right away."

Starr said goodbye and Oggie asked, "So where is it I'm takin' you two?"

She and Beau discussed what to do. They decided they'd get a rental to take them home—tomorrow, when the rental places opened up. Since tow fees to Casper would be astronomical, they'd call a towing company in Rawlins and have the Suburban hauled back there.

"How about a motel, then?" Starr suggested.

Oggie nodded. "A motel it is."

"What a damn mess," Beau mumbled.

"Sorry." Starr sighed.

Beau's armed tightened around her. "I wasn't blaming you. Your only mistake was coming along with me."

"There are no mistakes in this life," Oggie Jones intoned from the front seat. "Believe it. That girl is sittin' beside you at this exact minute because beside you is where she wants to be."

Beau muttered something about how old guys should mind their own business. Starr just cuddled closer and smiled.

Oggie Jones let them out in front of a Best Western motel. They thanked him and stood waving as the boat of a car drove away.

"What a guy," Starr murmured in admiration.

"Yeah," Beau agreed. "Got a mouth on him the size of the Grand Canyon." For that remark, he got an elbow in the ribs. "Hey!"

She grabbed his hand. "Let's get a room." She started for the glass door to the lobby.

He didn't budge. "One room? What about the hands-off rule?"

He *would* have to ask that. She let go of his hand. "You want your own room, is that it?"

"I was only saying—"

She didn't let him finish. "This is really not a problem. We'll get two beds instead of one. Fair enough?"

Shaking his head, he followed her inside.

The guy behind the desk had terry-cloth robes he could rent them, toothbrushes for sale—and a dryer they could use for their still-clammy clothes. By nine-thirty, their clothes were hung up in the closet nook off the bath in their room, all ready for tomorrow. They'd taken turns in the shower. Starr had made her call to Tess. They sat on their beds in their rented robes eating pepperoni pizza.

Once the pizza box was empty, Beau stretched out and grabbed the remote.

Now come on. What was this thing with guys and the remote? It had to be genetic. Ethan had it, and he wasn't even five. Beau lay back on his stacked pillows, surfing away, those muscular hairy legs crossed at the ankles.

Starr folded up the empty pizza box—slowly, with great care. Then she rose and put it in the wastebasket in the corner. She was working up the nerve, she told herself. In a minute or two, she'd ask him to turn it off, say they needed to talk.

He sent her a glance, a warm smile…and looked at the screen again, pointing the remote, switching to another channel.

It was nice, really. The two of them, safe and dry and warm. Together—even if they did have separate beds and he was watching TV. It felt…easy between them now. Companionable.

The way it *wouldn't* feel when she broke the news….

Maybe she'd brush her teeth first. Yeah. When in doubt as to how to tell a guy about the baby—get those teeth clean. The news about the baby might be the priority here. But dental hygiene was important, too.

She went to the vanity area between the closet nook and the bathroom and slithered the cellophane wrapper off the brush. The guy at the counter had provided a travel-sized toothpaste for free. She squeezed on a line of Crest and went to work.

Much better, she thought, once the job was done and her mouth felt minty-fresh. On the TV, the AFLAC duck was squawking. Beau chuckled.

Starr whirled from the sink and opened her mouth to speak.

But no.

Really, not now. Not right this minute. Let him relax for a while. It had been a rough day.

Under the rented robe she still wore her panties—and a souvenir T-shirt she'd bought from the guy at the front desk. It was extra-large. White, with an oil derrick spouting oil on the front and the words Casper Comes In A Gusher.

The perfect attire for a hands-off kind of night.

She removed the robe and hung it on a hanger—taking a lot more time than she needed to get it on there just right. She even tied the tie at the waist, so it wouldn't slip off and end up on the floor.

Once she had the robe hung up to her liking, she trotted over and meticulously folded the bedspread back to the bottom of the bed, smoothing out every wrinkle, getting the folds perfectly straight. Then she pulled back the covers and slid in. She fluffed up the pillows and made herself comfortable.

He was watching some nature show now. Baboons

grooming each other, a woman with an English accent talking in the background.

"Beau…"

He rolled his head her way and gave her a lazy smile. "Want to watch something else? Name it." He waved the remote at her. "We'll find it."

"I…" It just wasn't happening. She couldn't quite get it out. "Whatever. It's okay."

"Sure?"

I'm having your baby, Beau. "Yeah, really. This is fine…"

He hesitated, watching her. And then he shrugged and turned back to the screen again.

Well, she thought. Another opportunity royally blown. She looked at the ceiling for a while, thoroughly disgusted with herself. She was, she decided, the biggest coward in the whole wide world. Worse than that, she didn't intend to get one bit braver. Not tonight. She reached for the lamp switch. "Mind?"

"Not a problem." He turned the sound way down.

She switched off the light, lay back and closed her eyes. She'd get to it, she told herself. She would. Very soon…

At two-thirty in the morning—or so the digital clock on the nightstand said—Beau sat, wide-awake, in the dark. He'd switched off the TV hours ago, even though it was too damn quiet without it.

He could hear Starr breathing from the other bed, a tender little whisper of sound. Through the shadows, he could see the shape of her. She was turned on her side, facing the far wall, black hair spilling back, darker than the night itself, across the white pillow.

He let his gaze travel up the slope of her shoulder, slide down the sweet indentation of her waist, rise again at the soft swell of her hip....

He shouldn't have let her come with him on this disaster of a trip. He shouldn't even be seeing her, really. They should have left it alone after that night on the porch out at the cabin.

Hell, they probably shouldn't have even started up together in the first place. But they had. And now there were only a few days left and she would be gone. She wanted to share those days with him—and damn it to hell, he wasn't going to refuse her.

On the low dresser past the foot of the bed, against the opposite wall, he could see the envelope the lawyer had given him. Starr had taken it from her purse when she was digging around in there for a comb. She'd held it out to him, a shining look of hope on her beautiful face—that he'd open it, see what was in it.

Well, he wasn't going to open it. Not ever. He didn't need his daddy's old beat-up watch and his brother's battered wallet. He didn't need the keys to a truck that had been impounded and an apartment long ago rented to somebody else.

He'd carry it all on home with him, only because if he threw it in the trash right now, she just might pull it back out and insist that he take it with him—or go ahead and open it herself.

Uh-uh. Whatever she did if he tossed it out, there would be an argument.

He didn't need that. Not over the stuff T.J. used to carry in his pockets, not over something as meaningless like that.

And as for the things his brother had said...

Well, they were only the usual: *Pansy-ass loser.
Two-bit nobody. Chump cowhand. Idiot. Fool…*

She didn't need to hear it. Hell. Neither did he—
but it was better than a cigarette burn and a sharp knife
slicing, now wasn't it? And while he sat there in that
visitation booth and took what his brother dished out
to him, he held the knowledge that she waited for
him—safe, nowhere near that place—that when it was
over he could leave, go back to a good, honest life,
where he was straight with his neighbors and there
were people who trusted him.

It was like Starr had said. Some things you just had
to do. He felt a duty to go down there, now and then,
to listen to his rotten brother rant. It was a duty he
hated. It left him stupid and speechless with rage every
time. But he knew he'd end up doing it again before
T.J. finally ran out of appeals.

Starr sighed and moved beneath her blankets. She
turned over, so she faced his side of the room. Beau
sat as still as the headboard he leaned against. He
waited for her to settle in again.

But her breathing had changed. "Beau?" She
canted up on an elbow and reached for the lamp. He
shut his eyes against the burst of brightness. When he
opened them again, she was squinting at him. "God,
Beau. Don't you ever sleep?"

"Now and then."

She dragged herself up against the headboard. "It
can't be good for you, awake all the time," she grumbled. "People need their sleep."

"Yeah. Guess they do."

"Ugh." Grumpy and rumpled and so beautiful it
hurt to look at her, she shoved back the covers and

swung those long, smooth legs of hers to the floor. He got a flash of panty and didn't feel the least bit guilty for looking. "Water," she mumbled.

He admired the view of her walking away from him as she trudged around the end of her bed and over to the sink, where she grabbed a plastic cup and took a long drink. She set the cup down harder than she needed to and whirled on him, bracing a fist on her hip. "So are you ever going to tell me what went on with that brother of yours, what had you so mad you were driving seventy in the pouring rain on a narrow two-lane road?"

He could see by the determined gleam in her eye that she wasn't letting up on him until told her. And now he'd gotten a little time and distance from it, he figured he could probably talk about it without cursing a blue streak and breaking up the furniture. "Nothing much happened. He called me a bunch of names— whispering, keeping it low. He knows enough not to get the guards on him until he's finished reaming me a new one. I sat there and listened. He brought up how I turned on my own brothers, how I screwed him and Lyle, destroyin' their lives."

"That's sick and disgusting. And completely untrue."

"Maybe. But it's still his favorite subject when he gets me in to visit—how he wouldn't be where he is if it wasn't for me. Hell, to hear him tell it, Lyle wouldn't be dead. If they hadn't got arrested for rustling your dad's cattle—because *I* turned traitor to my own kin—Lyle wouldn't have been in jail where he got in that fight and got stabbed to the heart with a shiv filed down from a spoon."

She slapped a hand on the fake-marble sink counter. She had her lips pressed hard together and one hip stuck out, the oil derrick on her T-shirt pulsing with every angry breath she took. "That's totally ridiculous. You know that, don't you?"

He chuckled. "Yeah. But I still get mad enough to kick my own dog every time he does it to me."

"You know he's not worth your getting mad at."

"You bet I do—but I don't let the facts stop me. And the good news is, once I settle down, it's not really so bad. When I calm down enough to give it a little thought, I can see that at least the time's past when I would wet my pants in terror at the very thought that he might find a way to get out and come after me."

"He's never getting out," she said.

"Yeah," he answered dryly. "I suppose you're right—and the truth is, if T.J. found a way to come after me now, I'd fight back. One of us would end up dead."

"Him," she said, blood in her eye.

Beau chuckled. "You've never seen my brother fight. He fights dirty. There's a damn good chance he'd win. Lucky for me I'll never have to face that problem."

"But...that's all? He gets you down there to beat you up with words? To accuse you of doing what he and Lyle did to themselves?"

"That's about the size of it."

"Well then, Beau...why do you go?"

"You know, I was just sitting here in the dark asking myself that very same question...."

She waited for him to finish—tapping her bare foot,

adorable in her impatience. When he didn't go on, she demanded, "And?"

He lifted a shoulder in a shrug. "It's all he knows. He's not going to change. Good old Taft Eldridge will trot out a few more appeals and when that's all through with, they'll stick a needle in his arm—close the book on him, you could say. End of story. Lights out. He'll be off to join my daddy and Lyle in hell. They'll burn on together for all eternity."

She stood there, still fuming, waiting for more. When it didn't come she pushed away from the counter and marched over, ripe breasts bouncing under that silly shirt, and plopped herself down on the edge of his bed. Hauling one foot up, knee out so he had a good view of a nice stretch of milky-white inner thigh, she raked that gleaming, tangled black hair away from her forehead and let out a hard breath. "I'm sorry. There has to be more."

"There isn't."

"I don't believe you. There has to be something that keeps you going back."

He let his gaze wander up and down that thigh, his fingers just itching to reach out and stroke it. And his fingers weren't all that itched. If she turned around and looked down the blanket that covered his lower body, she'd see how happy he was to have her nearby. "You want me to keep hands off, you shouldn't be showing all that leg."

She only scowled at him. "Get a grip—and get back to the subject."

He bent a knee up, easing the ache a little—and masking the evidence of it. "You make it so *hard*."

She kept on scowling. "You aren't going to distract me from getting to the bottom of this."

He shifted on the pillows, canting his upper body her way, breathing through his nose, sucking in the jasmine scent of her. "There's nothing more to get to. We're at the bottom. He's a low-down rotten piece of human trash, my brother—but he *is* my brother. There's one thing I can do for him. I can listen while he trots out all the garbage. So I do."

"But what *good* does it do—him saying awful things to you, you sitting there and taking it?"

"Hell if I know. But as far as I can see, he's pretty much driven to do it. And I *can* take it. It's nothing to what he used to do. It's only words. I sit there and I let him say them. It's…what I'm willing to do."

She wasn't buying his reasoning. She looked at him sideways. "You're punishing yourself, aren't you?" Now flags of outraged color rode high on her velvet-soft cheeks. "Somewhere deep inside yourself, you *believe* what T.J. says to you. In your heart, you take the blame for everything, all the really bad stuff that happened in your family—your drunk, abusive daddy and your poor mom dying. Your brothers turning out the awful way they did…"

"No," he said. "No, I don't."

She yanked her shoulders back and faced him squarely. "And I don't believe you."

He looked at her flushed face, her flashing eyes—and the way that T-shirt showed the outline of her breasts. He could see her nipples.

Need for her slammed through him. Damn her and damn the knowledge in her eyes.

"You sit there," he said, his voice low and rough

as the sudden lust raging through him. "You sit there and tell me what I feel, how I am. Sit there in that shirt that shows off just about everything, driving me crazy with wanting you while you pick through my brain."

On her cheeks, the bright spots of color flamed all the redder. "That's what you think, huh?" She looked at him as if he'd just hauled off and punched her. "That's what you really believe this is about? Me teasing you while I dig out all your secrets? That's what you think I'm up to here?"

He was getting that ashy feeling in his mouth. That feeling a guy gets when he's been a total ass. "All right. Look. I'm outta line."

Her sweet face got softer. The mouth he loved quivered a little. "Who you gonna talk to, Beau? Who you gonna be honest with, if not with me? I'm the one who knows you, Beau. I'm the one who cares. You can go ahead, say no to me, say no to the life we might have shared. You can…deny me. And deny any truth I see about you. That's your right. I might even forgive you for all your denials, because I do know, I understand, the kind of things you've been through. Just…don't try to hurt me when all I did was to tell you the truth as I saw it. Don't attack me for saying what I really believe. Don't be mean or low-down. Leave that kind of stuff to T.J., all right?"

The last thing he had any right to do at that moment was to touch her. But he couldn't help himself. He reached out, pressed his palm to the achingly soft skin of her flushed cheek.

"Oh, Beau," she whispered, laying her own hand

over his. He felt her tremble, saw the tears that welled in those violet eyes.

He muttered, gruffly, "I don't know what the hell you see in me."

She sighed, cupping his hand in her smaller one, rubbing her cheek against his palm. "Well, and that's the basic problem, now isn't it?"

It hurt him—hurt bad. To see his own cruelty reflected back in her eyes.

He spread his fingers, letting hers slip between. Catching them, folding her fingertips into his palm, he gave a tug to pull her toward him. "Come on. Lie down with me...." She resisted, giving him a reproachful look as one tear escaped and slid along her cheek. He brushed that tear away with his free hand. "Just for a minute. You can stay outside the covers. I swear I won't put any moves on you."

"Oh, I don't think it's such a good idea."

"Come on..."

With a sigh she came down to him, the whole silky length of her pressing close to his side. He slipped his arm under her, so he could hold her closer still.

"Oh, Beau," she said low, her breath warm on his neck. "What am I going to do with you?"

He smiled to himself. He had a few ideas—not that he'd be acting on them. Uh-uh. They had a deal and he wouldn't go back on it, no matter how the feel and the womanly scent of her stirred him. He stroked her silky hair. "You might not believe this. I wouldn't blame you if you didn't. But I am grateful you came with me. I'm glad you're here."

She snuggled closer. "Well." She made a sniffing

sound and brushed at her nose. "That helps. It does...."

They were quiet together. It was good, just lying there with her tucked up close beside him. He tried to stay with that—with what was happening right now.

But still, the question that kept haunting him crept into his mind: How he would bear it when she was gone?

Four days left, counting this one newly begun a few hours ago. Four days and she was out of here. Out of his life. On to the career she'd worked so hard for, on to a whole different kind of life than he'd ever known.

He knew it was the right thing, to refuse her offer to stay here with him. It was the *only* thing, really. But that wasn't going to make her leaving any easier to take.

He'd see her again, now and then. When she came back home for visits with her family. Maybe they could go out....

But probably not. He had to be realistic. She'd have another life. She'd meet other men. She had it all: brains and drop-dead good looks and a willing heart. She wouldn't stay single forever. In the end, he'd be someone way back in her memory.

A guy she'd loved once, though it didn't work out....

"Beau?"

He kissed her hair. "Yeah?"

She had her hand on his chest, above the blanket, idly stroking. "Beau, I need to tell you something...."

Chapter Fifteen

"Beau," Starr whispered, "what would you say if…?"

Instead of finishing, she sighed.

Beau tried to dip his chin, to look at her. But she kept her head down. Her hand had stopped stroking, her fingers lay still over his heart.

He had the strangest feeling then, a kind of dread mingled with something else—a thread of hope, maybe. Which was stupid. Hope for what?

He prompted, "What would I say if…?"

She took forever to answer. In the silence he found himself realizing that she'd been doing that a lot. She'd look at him and start to talk—and then end up not saying anything. Or her gaze would shift away. When she finally spoke, he'd have the clear sense she wasn't saying what she'd started out to say.

"Oh, never mind," she said at last. "It's nothing...."

He wasn't sure about that. But he left it alone. What could it be but what had already been decided? She was leaving in four days. That wasn't going to change. Hashing it around some more wouldn't do either of them any good.

She stirred against him, sighing, settling in. In time, he heard her breathing even out, go shallow and slow. He waited a little longer, to make sure she was really asleep. Then he flipped the top blanket over her, so she wouldn't be cold.

A while after that, he gently pulled his arm from under her neck and reached over her to turn off the light. Starr mumbled something—his name, it sounded like—but she didn't wake up. He eased himself back in next to her and gathered her close, brushing the lightest of kisses against the crown of her head.

Starr slept on. Beau stared into the darkness, holding her sweet body close, thinking that there were worse ways to spend a sleepless night.

They got up at eight and walked over to the coffee shop next to the motel for breakfast. By ten, Starr had arranged to have the Suburban towed to a Rawlins repair shop. She'd also called her insurance company. The adjustor would visit the repair shop in the next few days—most likely not till after the holiday—and determine whether the vehicle was worth fixing. Her dad had her set up with a roadside service plan that included a free rental if she needed one, so she called Avis and they sent over a car. The car arrived at ten-thirty. Beau settled up the motel bill and they took off, with Beau at the wheel.

It was a nice ride home, for the most part. The sun shone bright in a clear blue sky and it was four-lane interstate the whole way to Medicine Creek. They talked easily about casual things. Three times during the two-hour trip, she started to tell him about the baby.

He'd glance over when she cleared her throat, or said his name. She'd look in his eyes and the words would die on her lips.

It was like a bad habit, really—a bad habit in reverse. The more you smoked, the more you *had* to smoke. The more she didn't tell Beau about the baby, the more she *couldn't*.

The third time she started in and didn't finish, he remarked on it. "You've been doing that a lot lately—starting to say something, then holding it back. If there's something you need to say, maybe you'd better just go ahead and say it."

It was the closest she was ever going to get to an invitation. Her heart raced and her palms went clammy. She rubbed her hands on her jeans and cleared her throat some more—and despised herself utterly when, once again, all she managed to get out was, "I…well, I'm going miss you, that's all."

He seemed to buy it—to accept that her regret at leaving him was all she had on her mind. "It's the best thing," he said softly, eyes on the road ahead. "The *right* thing…"

She wanted to reach over and whack him upside the head about then. "No, it's not. It's not the best thing, it's not even the *right* thing. It's just how you want it because you had a bad start in life and you've convinced yourself you can't deal with being a husband or a dad.''

He glanced her way again. ''I think I'll just keep my mouth shut on this one.''

''Good idea,'' she muttered. She folded her arms over her middle and watched the golden prairie rolling by, the bluffs in the distance, the shadows where the land dipped to coulees and draws. No way she was going to light into him—even if he was a thick-headed fool determined to throw away the best thing that had ever happened to either of them because he insisted on blaming himself for tragedies that weren't in any way his fault.

Her fury was at least half guilt over her own cowardice. She knew that. But it didn't make her one bit less ready to chew nails. They rode along in silence the rest of the way, the storm inside her kind of blowing itself out.

By the time she let him off at Daniel's place, she was able to lean across the seat and give him quick kiss goodbye—and to drag the now-battered yellow envelope out of her purse. ''Don't forget this.'' He'd abandoned it on the dresser in the motel room and she'd snatched it up at the last minute. The look on his face as she handed it over told her he hadn't left it behind by accident.

''Thanks,'' he muttered, scowling.

''My pleasure.'' She gave him her sweetest smile. ''Drop by my place tonight?''

His expression lightened. ''I'll be there.'' He got out and she went around and slid in behind the wheel.

At the Rising Sun, they were just serving the midday meal at the main house when she stopped in to tell everyone she was home safe.

Edna jumped up from the table. "Have you eaten? Sit down, I'll get you a plate."

So she ate a little and apologized to her dad and Tess for wrecking the Suburban. "I think, since it's six years old and all, they'll probably declare it totaled. I'm sorry about that. I know it had a lot of sentimental value."

Tess looked at her husband, fond memories in her eyes. "I had this ancient Tercel—remember, Zach?"

Her dad's eyes got right next door to misty. "I do."

"I was never so touched as when your father drove me up to Sheridan to pick up that Suburban—but in the end, the car itself is just a way to get from here to there. The important thing is that you and Beau came out of it without a scratch."

"Wasn't your fault, anyway," her dad added. "I'm just grateful that deer didn't come flying through the windshield."

"Ain't that the truth," old Tim piped up. "A deer's gonna do what a deer's gonna do—including jumping right in front of you out of nowhere on a rainy road."

The way he said that had her thinking of the sweet old coot who'd given them a ride. She told them all about Oggie Jones, about his chewed-up cigar and his ratty suspenders, his antique Cadillac with all that stuff in the trunk. "Such a strange old guy," she said. "He talked nonstop all the way to Casper...."

"Sounds like a real character," her dad agreed.

After they ate, Tess volunteered to follow Starr up to the airport in Sheridan where she could drop of the rental car. "We can stop in for groceries on the way back."

But Starr shook her head. "I get a better deal on it if I take the weekly rate. So I can just drive it up there when I go to the airport on Tuesday."

"Come with me, anyway," Tess insisted. "It'll be our last chance for a little time together before you're off to New York."

"Go," Edna chimed in. "Ethan and I can look after things here."

"Shopping?" Ethan licked off his milk mustache and plunked down his glass. "I like shopping. I'm going, too."

"I'm baking cookies. Chocolate chip," Edna wheedled. "I could sure use some help...."

Ethan considered. "Who gets to lick the bowl?"

"Well, whoever stays and helps me."

Ethan agreed to stay. And Starr said she'd go to Sheridan with Tess. "But I should call Jerry first..."

Tomorrow was Saturday—and Monday was the final holiday of the summer. So she apologized to her boss for not being there her last day of work. "And I promise I'll get you one more installment of Mabel's column before I leave."

"You change your mind about life in the big city," Jerry suggested for about the tenth time that summer, "you come on back home and take the job that's waiting for you right here."

"I will," she said, wishing that could happen, but doubting it ever would. Yeah, she'd realized she could make a home here and be happy. But without Beau?

No. She'd rather just go ahead, stick with her original plan, make a new life in a place where there were fewer reminders of what could never be.

Once she got up the nerve to tell them her problem, Tess and her dad were going to start in on her. They'd argue that she'd be better off at home where they could help her with the baby. But she'd deal with that conversation when she got to it—which wasn't going to be until after she'd told Beau.

And telling Beau? When would she manage that?

At the rate she was going, not for a long time.

Once Starr had called Jerry, she and Tess headed for Sheridan and the Safeway there.

Starr pushed the cart. Tess read from a long list, pulling boxes and jars off the shelves, stacking everything neatly in the cart as Starr rolled it up and down the aisles. Starr watched her stepmother, the way she would frown at her list and then look up, scanning the shelves, seeking just the brand and size she wanted. Tess looked better every day, Starr thought. Her step seemed a little lighter, her voice had more of the old lilt in it. The dark smudges were gone from under her eyes.

It never occurred to Starr they'd run into trouble in the aisle with the baby supplies. Really, she didn't even notice what was in that aisle. They only turned down that way because Tess had a few things she wanted at the other end.

Starr saw all the baby stuff up ahead and tried walking faster. It didn't work. Tess slowed at a vertical row of teething rings and pacifiers, each one individually packed on a cardboard backing and hanging from a line of hooks.

"Oh, my…" Tess unhooked a teething ring from the row and turned to Starr, who'd backed up reluctantly to wait for her. "Can you believe, three weeks ago, I bought one of these? I thought it was so cute, I couldn't resist it, even though I knew the baby wouldn't be needing it for quite a while." The ring was a toy doughnut—complete with plastic icing and sprinkles. Tess was shaking her head. "Now, isn't that silly? I should have brought it back for a refund. What good is a fake doughnut-teething ring going to do anybody now?"

It hurt, just to look at her. The pain in her eyes went down and down, as if there was no bottom to it.

For Tess, Starr realized, that pain would never completely fade. There would always be a tender, sad place in her secret heart for the baby she'd wanted so much, the baby who never got a chance to be born….

Starr opened her mouth to say how they ought to get moving. What came out was, "Well, I guess you can give it to me."

Chapter Sixteen

Tess dropped the teething ring.

Neither of them moved to pick it up. The two of them just stood there, next to the bright bottles of baby lotion, the big packages of disposable diapers, the shelf of bibs and rattles and little tub toys, staring at each other.

"'Scuse me," said a voice behind Starr.

"Oh," said Starr. "Sure." She angled the cart out of the way and the other shopper rolled by.

The spell-like silence broken, Tess bent and picked up the teething ring. She hung it back on its hook. When she turned to Starr again she asked, very carefully, "Is it true. Are you—?"

"Yeah," Starr cut her off before she said the word. "Yeah. I am."

That got them both staring at each other again. Starr

had the strangest feeling—as if any minute she would turn to glass. And shatter.

Tess said, "Maybe we should just finish the shopping. We can talk when we get in the car."

Starr gripped the cart handle. Hard, with both hands. She couldn't believe she'd just popped out with it like that. "All of a sudden, I feel kind of sick...."

Tess stepped close and spoke softly. "What can I do? You need to sit down?"

Starr swallowed, took a slow, deep breath and let it out with care. "I...I'm okay. I'll be okay."

"Sure?"

"Uh. Yeah. Yeah, I'm sure." She straightened her shoulders. "It was just...the shock, you know? Of getting it out there."

"Does Beau...?"

Starr shook her head. "He doesn't know."

"Oh, honey..."

Starr bit the inside of her lip to make it stop quivering. "If you look at me like that, I'm just going to burst into tears right here in Safeway—either that, or throw up. And then we'll never get this shopping done."

"I shouldn't have told you," Starr said. They had the groceries loaded up and Tess was driving them home. "Not yet, anyway. Not until I told Beau."

Tess sent her a look of complete understanding. "It's hard. I know...." Something in her tone, in the way her voice trailed off, made Starr sit up and take notice.

"You do know? I mean, *really* know?"

Tess nodded, her eyes on the road. "I was younger,

though. Only seventeen. Not even through high school yet…''

"Oh, God. Jobeth?"

Tess nodded again and sent Starr another look. "Someday we can have a long talk about what a tough time I had. But it's not important right now. Right now, we're talking about you."

"Great." Starr stared at the dashboard.

"Come on. Talk to me…"

So Starr brought Tess up to speed: how far along she was, when she'd taken the test.

Tess hit the gas and passed a truck loaded high with rolls of barbwire. "Those tests are pretty reliable."

"Ninety-nine point four percent. Or so the box said."

"And now…?"

Starr shrugged. "I'll go to New York on Tuesday. I know that much. I'm not sure yet how long I'll stay, or how I'm going to feel about being there when I get too big to work. I'm figuring I'll manage somehow." Her job wouldn't pay all that much—especially not at first. But there was always her trust money. It was plenty. And she'd have Grandmother Elaine and Grandpa Travis nearby. She doubted they'd bat an eye at her news. They were very…progressive. They traveled in the kind of circles where people had babies all the time without getting married first. It was kind of a joke in the family, really, that their only son was so conservative—and that he'd grown up wanting nothing more than to get back to Wyoming and run the family ranch.

Tess asked, "And after the baby comes?"

"I just...don't know yet. Right now I'm kind of taking it one day at a time."

"But you do know you want to keep the baby?"

They looked at each other. There were tears in Tess's eyes. Starr felt her own tears rising, tightening her throat. "Can we just not start bawling, okay?"

Tess swallowed and nodded and looked at the road. "Okay, then. You're keeping your baby...."

"Yes. I am."

"And since you're going ahead to New York, I'm taking it you don't want to marry Beau?"

Dear God. Beau again. "Look. I told him I loved him, that I wanted to stay here, to get married and maybe build a house next to Daniel's. All of it, what people do when they love each other and want to be together...."

"And?"

"He won't. He says he's never getting married. He's got...issues, when it comes to things like marriage and having kids."

"Issues?" Tess wrinkled her nose as if the word had a suspicious smell.

"Yeah. Issues. Issues about all that old garbage with his family, with his mean, drunk father and his abusive brothers. All that."

"But he loves you," Tess said, as if that solved everything. "Any fool can see that."

"Maybe so."

"No *maybe* about it. He does."

"Well, for Beau, I guess it's just not a question of love."

"And that is plain idiotic. It's *always* a question of love. Why do people *do* these things to themselves—

to each other?'' Tess was shaking her head again. ''Take your father and me. We were such fools. We told ourselves our marriage was for practical reasons. He needed a good wife, someone like me—a good worker, a woman accustomed to the ranching life. And I needed…security, a stable home where I could do a decent job of raising Jobeth. It took me longer than it should have to realize what I really wanted from him. And then it took *him* even longer to believe me.''

Starr wasn't surprised. ''I kind of figured it was something like that.''

''It was love I really needed from your dad—and it was love that he needed from me. I should have known it from the first. Love can…heal a lot of hurt, you know?''

''Yeah. So everyone says.'' Starr turned away. She stared out her side window, toward Cloud Peak capped in white in the distance.

Tess made a low sound in her throat. ''So…you told Beau you love him and want to marry him.''

''That's right.''

''But not about the baby.''

Starr put up both hands. ''So okay, shoot me. I did it all backward. I had some idea that it would be better to tell him I loved him and I wanted to stay *before* I told him I was having his baby. It didn't work out so well.''

Tess tapped the steering wheel—hard—with the heel of her hand. ''That man. What an idiot. Anyone can see he worships you. *Issues* or not, I can't believe he wouldn't jump at the chance for a life with you.''

''Believe it. Not only did he *not* jump, he turned me down flat.''

"But surely he'll change his mind—when you tell him."

"Maybe. I guess so. But what will that be about? Him marrying me because he feels he has to? Oh, I don't think so."

They rode along in silence for a while. Finally, Tess said, "I believe in Beau, I truly do. I think when you tell him, he'll do the right thing."

"Great. We'll see about that, won't we?" *In a hundred years, when I finally get the words out.*

"But, Starr…"

"What?"

"If, for whatever reason, it doesn't work out with Beau, I hope you'll consider coming home—for a while anyway—when the baby's born. Let us help you, at least in those first months when your baby is going to be a full-time job. Your father and I would—"

Starr put up a hand. "I'm just not there yet. I can't…think that far ahead."

Tess seemed about to argue, but then she only said, "Okay. I understand."

"And please. Don't tell Dad. I'll do it myself. When I'm ready."

Tess didn't answer for the longest time. When she did speak, it wasn't anything Starr wanted to hear. "Your father and I don't keep secrets from each other—oh, maybe now and then. When it's a confidence that doesn't affect him, or me, or the family. Starr, honey, this isn't that kind of secret."

Starr was shaking her head. Vehemently. What had possessed her to go and open her big mouth? She should have known Tess would have trouble keeping something like this from her dad. "Dad can't know until I've told Beau. I…oh, I shouldn't have even told *you*. It was stupid." She shook her head some more. "Dumb, dumb, dumb…"

"Shh," said Tess. She reached across the seat and patted Starr's arm.

Starr wasn't about to be soothed—not about this. "I mean it, Tess. You might be my stepmother, but that's not why I told you. I told you because you're my friend. I love Dad. You love Dad. But you know how he is. The way he's gonna see it, the only problem here is I haven't told Beau I'm having his baby—so Beau can do the right thing and get a ring on my finger. If Dad knows…uh-uh. He's too likely to butt in, to try to 'fix' things. And this isn't something he can fix. This is *my* problem. My problem and Beau's…"

"But you haven't *told* Beau."

Starr slumped in the seat. "Oh, rub it in some more, why don't you?"

Tess watched the road ahead, frowning.

What a mess, Starr was thinking. "I'm sorry. To put you in the middle of this. I shouldn't have said anything."

Tess shook her head. "No. I want to know about something like this. I'm proud that you trust me."

"You just have to accept that this isn't six years ago. I'm all grown up now. It's my decision—who to tell and what to do."

"Beau's the one you need to tell."

Starr let out a groan. "How many times are you going to say that?"

"You're angry."

"No. I'm just…frustrated. Really, really frustrated. And I'm hurt. I told Beau I *loved* him, Tess. And it didn't do a bit of good." The damn tears rose up again. Starr sniffed them back.

Watching the road, Tess fumbled in the console and yanked out a tissue. "Here."

"Thanks." Starr blew her nose and dabbed at her eyes.

And Tess gave in. "Okay. I'll keep my mouth shut. I'll let you tell your dad yourself, when you're ready to. I do respect your right to do this your way."

Beau arrived at the cabin at a little after seven that night. Flushed with new purpose to get the words out, Starr got a beer for him and they sat out on the steps. They watched the night come, just sitting there, being together….

He left around nine.

She hadn't told him.

Saturday, they went up to Sheridan for dinner and a movie. She had a lovely time.

And she didn't say a word about the secret she was keeping from him.

Sunday evening, in Patriot Park, the town merchants gave the second—and last—outdoor dance of the summer. Beau took Starr. They danced together, one dance after another. She swayed in his arms and thought about how the summer was all but over now. It had gone by much too fast.

Daniel was there. He sat at the Bravos' table. When Beau and Starr joined the group to sit out a dance, they learned that Nate had called the Rising Sun just as Zach and Tess were leaving for the park. Meggie was up at Memorial—in labor. Starr and Tess shared a glance across the table. Starr was the one who looked away.

Beau took her back to the cabin at a little after one. "I'll drop by tomorrow to say goodbye...."

"I'd like that."

He kissed her, a long, slow kiss. She kissed him back. By the time they pulled apart, they were both breathing hard.

"Better go," he said.

"Yeah. Guess you'd better..."

Starr went inside and stood at the sink and stared at her shadowy reflection in the dark windowpane. Tomorrow night would be it. She'd have to do it then or it wouldn't get done before she left for New York.

The next morning, she went over to the main house for breakfast. The phone rang as they were sitting down. Her dad answered it.

When he hung up, he had wide smile on his craggy face. "That was Nate. It's a girl."

After she helped with the dishes, Starr called around to the neighbors, gathering the local news. She sat down to write Mabel's column.

It's a girl this time for Nate and Megan Bravo. The little darling was born at 4:03 a.m., Saturday, August 30. Sarah Ellen Bravo is 19 inches tall and 8 pounds, 3 ounces. Welcome to the world, Sarah Ellen—and congratulations, Nate and Meggie!

After she finished the column and e-mailed it off, Starr shared the midday meal with the family and then returned to the cabin to pack. She had her suitcases ready and waiting in the rental car when Beau arrived at six.

She opened the door to his knock and the sight of him standing there, broad-shouldered and so handsome, his hat in his hands…it was almost too much for her.

She knew at that moment that she wasn't going to tell him—not tonight. Not before she left.

In their motel room in Casper, he had talked about willingness. He'd said that visiting his brother and taking T.J.'s abuse was what he was willing to do.

Well, this was about willingness, too. Right now, she simply was *not.*

Not willing to tell him. Not willing to deal with his reaction—whatever it would end up being—when he found out there was a baby coming.

Yeah, she was a stinking coward. So what? It could wait a few months. She'd be home for Thanksgiving. She'd tell him then.

Or maybe at Christmas…

What did it matter, really, *when* she told him? It wasn't as if she was running away and never coming back. She'd be home now and then and eventually, during one of her visits, she'd get around to it. In five or six months, she could just point to her stomach. *Hey, Beau. Guess what?*

That would do it. About as simple and direct as you could get.

Her misery must have shown in her face. "Bad idea, huh," he said, his voice low and rough, "for me to come by tonight?"

What was there to say?

Nothing. Not a damn thing.

She reached out her hand, grabbed his wrist and pulled him inside, hitting the door so it slammed shut behind him.

"Starr," he said, blinking down at her, bewildered, "I don't—"

"No words." She put her hands flat on his chest and she shoved him back against the door. "Just...no words. Okay?"

Chapter Seventeen

Starr surged up against him, pressing that sweet body of hers all along the front of him. Beau went rock-hard in that instant, his manhood straining at his jeans.

What the hell was up with her? He didn't get it—and she wasn't saying.

He looked down at her soft mouth. She was holding it up, offering it to him.

Well, fine. Did she think he'd have some argument with that? With a low groan, he brought his mouth down hard on hers, invading, demanding.

She didn't object to his roughness, not in the least. She kissed him right back, hard as he was kissing her. Her hand slid down his arm, taking his hat away, sending it sailing....

Where did it land? He didn't see—and he didn't care. She was already working at the buttons of his shirt.

Beau groaned into her mouth and took hold of the tight little T-shirt she wore. He yanked it upward.

With a moan, she raised her arms. He whipped that shirt over her head and tossed it off to join his hat.

He grabbed for her then, wrapping his arms around her, around all that womanly softness. He kissed her for all he was worth as his hands roamed her back, finding the double hook that held her bra, working at it until it gave.

He slid the straps down her arms. She shrugged free of them. He got the bra completely off her and he tossed it away.

She melted in close to him again. He gathered her in, one hand at her upper back, pressing, so he could feel those full breasts of hers, the nipples hard little points against his chest. With his other hand, he cupped her bottom, bringing her up and into him, bucking his hips against her, groaning at the sweet agony it caused him.

She was…on fire. Liquid fire, blazing in his arms. Her mouth burned under his, branding him….

They kissed as if they would never stop, as if they would eat each other alive, standing right there at the door. She got all the buttons of his shirt undone and she shoved it over his shoulders and down his arms. He yanked his hands free—and she whipped his shirt away.

She let go of his mouth, her soft lips sliding downward, her teeth nipping his chin. That naughty tongue of hers trailed along his throat. He groaned in the wake of it. Her breath was ragged and hot against his skin. Moaning, he dropped his head back. It hit the door with a hard, knocking sound. He didn't care. He moaned some more.

Down she went, nipping and licking along the center of his chest. And lower.

She sank to her knees in front of him.

Beau braced his boots a little wider for balance as she reached his belly. She lingered there, black hair a gleaming spill over her shoulders, over the curves of her perfect breasts, as she burned a row of wet kisses along the top of his jeans, her tongue dipping into his navel, her busy fingers working at the button of his fly.

She ripped that fly open. The zipper hissed down. And then she slid her fingers up the sides of his thighs, a burning pressure along the line of his hips, clearing the barrier of denim at last, fingerpads pressing flesh. A long, hot shiver ran through him when she dipped those fingers under the waist of his jeans. Her nails scored his hips as she dragged downward—too fast.

His arousal caught on the elastic of his briefs. He groaned louder than ever with the agonizing combination of pleasure and pain.

She made little cooing, soothing sounds as—gently now—she guided the elastic out of the way. She…licked him. One long, slow swipe of that wet tongue of hers.

And then her warm, smooth, knowing fingers closed around him, squeezing him. He felt himself kick against her palm and a strangled groan escaped his lips.

The pleasure was too intense. His head jerked back again, hitting the door harder than the first time.

She said his name then, "Beau…" And once more. "Beau…" in two haunting, rough whispers of sound.

That soft mouth closed around him.

Beau thought he would die—die and be glad to go. Her fingers moved lower—taunting, teasing, cupping, rubbing—driving him stark raving out of his mind. Her mouth?

Her mouth still had him, holding him. It was…so wet. So hot…sliding along him, taking him in, slowly letting him out…

He grabbed her by the shoulders. "Wait," he growled. And then he swore.

She lifted her head then, tossing that black hair back away from her angel's face. Her eyes gleamed, jewel-like, behind drooping, lazy lids. Her mouth was bruised and wet and deepest red with what she'd been doing to him. Her breath came ragged. Her full breasts had a soft pink flush across them. Her nipples were tight little buds…

"Wait," he said again. If she didn't stop, he would lose it right there.

He hauled her up, along the length of him, getting her across the shoulders and under the knees and hoisting her high against his chest. He kissed her. She gave that kiss back to him, hungry and eager, whimpering low in her throat.

He started walking.

He carried her across the room, turning sideways to get through the slit between the two curtains. Once in there, he set her down on the end of the bed.

She scooted backward, switching on the lamp, kicking off her sandals, shoving down her jeans. He dropped to the edge of the bed and got rid of his boots and his socks, then stood again to get his jeans off the rest of the way.

Finally, they were both naked. He went down to her, rolling her under him, slamming his mouth down on hers, sucking until she gave him her tongue.

As he kissed her, he stuck an arm out and fumbled for the bed stand, finding the small drawer in the front of it, sliding it open, feeling inside…

He got out the foil-wrapped square and lifted his mouth from hers to catch the corner between his teeth.

She opened her eyes and looked at him. She had the strangest expression on her face. He couldn't figure it. What was she thinking? Those shining eyes spoke of mysteries a mere man would never understand. She shook her head at him and a tiny smile curved her lips.

He stared down at her, drowning in those knowing eyes, hurting with the need to have her softness all around him.

She brought her hand up between them, took the little package from him. Her small, white teeth flashed as she neatly tore off the top strip. Her fingers swift and knowing, she had it free of the package and sliding down over him in no time at all.

And then, her hand curled warm and sure around him, she guided him home.

He pressed in and she took him. All the way. Her body gloved him, tight and wet and so right.

It was perfect. So exactly, so absolutely right…

He looked down at her, at her wild, black hair tangled on the pillow, at her lazy, gleaming amethyst eyes. At her secret smile that seemed to hint at things he'd never get a chance to know.

Stay, he thought. *Never leave me…*

He would have said it, too. But he stopped himself just in time, lowering his mouth to hers instead, using a kiss to seal his lips against the words he knew had no right to say.

They moved together. He shut his eyes and let the wonder take him.

She angled sideways, pushing, urging him to his back. They were rolling. She took the top position, her upper body rising above him as below she rocked him on.

He dared to open his eyes and look at her, at her body arching, her hair a wild black halo around that face that would forever haunt his dreams.

He grabbed her hips and surged up into her. She flung her head back, moaning his name.

At midnight, he slid from the bed, found his jeans and his boots and put them on.

"Beau?" She held up her arms to him.

He bent close. She wrapped those warm, soft arms around him and he pressed his lips to hers one last time—a final kiss so sweet and tender, it sent a deep ache of longing all through him.

When he lifted his head she said, "Goodbye, Beau." He started to speak, but she stopped him with her fingers to his lips. "Goodbye."

What more was there to say? He cupped her sweet face and looked at her in the glow from the bedside lamp, memorizing anew every line, every soft, amazing curve.

In the end, she had to take his hands and gently push them away.

He rose and left the bed, stepping through the curtain, pausing on the other side of it, hands fisted at his sides, longing only to go back.

Knowing he wouldn't.

When he had himself under sufficient control, he collected his shirt and his hat and went out the door, closing it quietly behind him.

Chapter Eighteen

"I see you are doing very nicely, very nicely indeed," Dr. Zibovian said. Starr looked up at the doctor who was smiling and running knowing brown hands over Starr's exposed—and slightly rounded—belly. "You may sit up now." Starr pushed herself up and pulled the sides of the pink paper smock so it covered the front of her. Dr. Zibovian scribbled notes on her clipboard. "Headaches?"

"They seem to have faded away the past couple of weeks. And my face isn't breaking out anymore." That had started about two weeks after she arrived in New York. She'd felt thirteen again—and not in a good way. But now, in early November, as she moved into her fourth month of pregnancy, her skin was clear again.

"Hmm. Yes. Excellent. Yes." Round brown eyes

met Starr's again. "You are eating well, taking your vitamins?" Starr nodded. "Keeping stress to a minimum?"

She thought of her boss at *CityWide*, Diana LeBond. Diana could run her ragged. But other than that—and the ache in her heart for a certain stubborn cowboy… "Doing my best."

"Your blood work is normal, urine sample looks fine. I'm seeing no edema. Good. Very good. Questions?"

They talked for a few minutes more, then Starr got dressed, stopped in at the front desk to settle up, and took the elevator down to the lobby. Luck was with her. She stepped out onto West Fifty-Ninth Street just as a cab slid to the curb and a sweet-faced elderly lady got out. Starr took the cab to her apartment in a gorgeous Deco building on West Eighty-Sixth.

Starr loved where she lived. The apartment had all the other editorial assistants at the office green with envy. She had a view of Central Park out her living room window, hardwood floors throughout and 700 square feet of living space. Yeah, the place listed for considerably more than her salary. But since her grandmother owned the building, the rent was no problem—there was none.

The phone was ringing as she let herself in the door. Starr ran to get it. She checked the display. Yes! Tess. Tess called two or three times a week and Starr was always glad to hear her voice.

She grabbed the phone. "Hi."

"Just get in?"

"Uh-huh." Starr got a can of pear juice—lately she

had a thing for pear juice—from the fridge and popped the top. She took a long sip. "Went for my checkup."

"And?"

"Lookin' good."

"Oh, I can't wait to see you. Only three weeks to go…"

Starr set her juice can on the counter and looked out her kitchen window at the fire escape and the gray wall of the building next door. Good a time as any to break the bad news. "Well, I've been meaning to tell you…" Starr let her voice trail off.

Tess got the message—and didn't like it. "Oh, no. Honey, it's Thanksgiving. We all want to see you."

"And I want to see you. But, well, you know how it is with flights these days. Always delays. I'll probably get stuck in Denver, like I did on the way out here. I'll get home—and then just have turn around and come back."

Tess let out a hard sigh. "It's Beau, isn't it?"

"No. No, not at all." It was an outright lie.

And Tess was no fool. "He needs to know."

Starr laughed at that one. It was not a very cheerful sound. "Coulda fooled me."

"*Other* people are going to have to know as well." Tess kind of whispered that one—as if she feared someone might be listening in. "By Christmas you'll definitely be showing. Do you realize that?"

Might as well get all the bad news over with at once. "See, the thing about Christmas is the same as the thing about Thanksgiving. I don't have any leave built up yet, and I'll only get a couple of days…"

She could close her eyes and picture Tess so clearly about now. She'd be in the big east-facing master bedroom, slowly sinking to the edge of the bed she shared with Starr's dad. "No. No, now this isn't right."

"Tess, I have a new job. I can't just take off for a week or two because it's a holiday. It doesn't work like that—and let's not argue over this. Let's—"

"No." Tess's soft voice had a thread of steel in it now. "No, I think we need to talk about it. I think we need to talk about responsibility—and how you keep running away from it."

"But I'm not running away. I'm right here. And I *will* be coming home."

"When?"

"Eventually."

Tess wasn't going for it. "Starr, you have got to tell Beau about that baby. It isn't right that you—"

"I *will* tell him."

"When?"

"I said. Eventually."

"That is no answer."

"Tess, this is my problem. Let me deal with it my own way."

"But you're *not* dealing with it. And you are putting me in the position of lying to your father every single day."

"Look. There's no point in going on and on about this. I'm sorry, but I'm not coming home for Thanksgiving—or for Christmas."

"You can't go on like this."

"Watch me."

They argued for a while longer. When they said goodbye, nothing had been solved.

Starr took the rest of her pear juice and went over to the window that looked out on the park. It was beautiful out there, the trees aflame with the colors of fall. Starr stared at all that beauty and muttered rude things under her breath.

Tess didn't get it. She just couldn't understand. Damn it, it wasn't fair. Starr was doing her best, taking care of herself and her coming baby—eating right, going to bed early…

What more did Tess want from her?

Starr drained the last of her juice and wandered back to the kitchen area to toss the can in the bin under the sink. She kicked the cabinet door closed and leaned on the counter and stared out the window at that brick wall.

Slowly, as she gazed blindly at the gray-painted brick, the truth settled over her.

All her muttered excuses and self-justifications didn't change the facts. In the end, she would have to take her broken heart and her expanding tummy and go home for the holidays.

Tess was right. And Starr knew it.

What Starr didn't know was that her father and the hands had come in a little early that day.

Zach took off his coat and boots in the laundry room and climbed the stairs in his stocking feet. He heard his wife talking on the phone in their bedroom and before he pushed open the half-shut door, he heard her say, "Starr, you have got to tell Beau about that baby."

Zach waited, there in the hall, on the other side of that half-open door until his wife hung up the phone. And then he gave that door a shove—not too hard.

Just enough that it swung all the way inward and Tess could see him standing there.

The wind blew the first cold flakes of snow against his face as Beau shut the gate between the two small pastures. The calves on one side of the fence bawled for their mamas. The cows on the other side bellowed back at them.

Tomorrow, they'd run them all into the corrals nearby and put them through the squeeze chute to medicate them for grubs. Then they'd drive the cows down to the southern pasture for the winter.

The calves they'd leave right here. Over the following few days, the calves would forget their mothers and learn to eat cattle cake. Then they'd be ready to be trucked farther out to their winter home.

No calf liked it when you took its mama away. But they got used to it soon enough.

Too bad a man couldn't be more like a calf. Too bad he couldn't just accept what he wasn't gonna have and get on with his life.

Too bad in the middle of the night he couldn't stop himself from thinking he smelled jasmine, couldn't help wishing he could turn and look over at the empty spot next to him and find a certain black-haired woman lying there, fast asleep, all wrapped in dreams.

The pain of missing her wasn't getting any better. He was starting to accept the fact that it never would, starting to admit to himself that the day was gonna come—and soon—that he'd get himself on a plane and head for New York City.

He wouldn't be going as a tourist.

He'd be going to try to get back the woman he'd sent away.

And come to think of it, there was another way that a calf was different from a man. A calf didn't get any choice in the matter. When weaning time came, a calf had to grow up.

A man, on the other hand, was a free agent. He could act like a damn baby his whole life long if he chose to.

Yeah. Those nights alone had given him way too much time to think, given him time to accept the fact that the hard things Starr had said to him—about his family, about how, deep down, he'd always blamed himself for the way things turned out—they were all true...

"Let's get back to the house," Daniel shouted against the bawling of the cattle and the rising wind. "Get some food in our bellies...."

Beau mounted up. He and Daniel and the two temporary hands they'd hired just before gathering day turned their horses for home. The ride didn't take long.

When they reached the house, there was a Rising Sun pickup waiting in the yard. Zach got out as Beau dismounted.

Chapter Nineteen

Two days after her argument with Tess, Starr called her stepmother to say she'd be home for Thanksgiving, after all.

Tess acted kind of strange, really. Kind of…distant in a pleasant sort of way.

"I'm glad to hear it," she said. "It's the right thing and I'm so happy you're coming home…."

There was something kind of canned about it—about her tone of voice, about the by-rote way she said the words. As if whatever she was really thinking wasn't getting said.

"Tess. Is something wrong?"

"Well, no. Of course not. I'm pleased you're coming. I truly am."

Starr hung up and got on the Internet to look for a flight. She was scanning the options, trying to find one that wouldn't have her hanging around in Denver for three hours, when the lobby intercom buzzer rang.

It was the doorman. "Ms. Bravo. There's a Beau Tisdale down here to see you. Should I send him up?"

Her knees suddenly gone to jelly, Starr leaned against the wall and tried to answer. Her lips moved, but no sound came out.

"Ms. Bravo. Are you there?"

"I...uh..." Her mouth was so dry. And her stomach was churning. "Yes, Andy," she croaked. "Go ahead. Send him up."

Starr staggered to the couch. She was still sitting there, trying to breathe normally, trying not to throw up, when the doorbell rang.

She didn't move. Funny, she wasn't quite sure she could trust herself to get up.

The bell rang again. *I can't. I just can't do this,* she told herself silently. Still, somehow, she slowly rose.

About halfway to the door, she put it together: Tess's distant attitude, Beau showing up at her door out of nowhere....

The door opened at last. "What a surprise," Starr said.

Damn, she was beautiful, Beau thought. Too bad she looked mad enough to kick a porcupine barefooted.

"Come on in," she said in a tone that clearly told him she meant, *go to hell.*

So much for a sweet and tender reunion.

Beau picked up his duffel and followed her through a short, narrow entrance hall into a nice-size living area.

She pointed at the duffel he still clutched in his fist. "Just...put it down there." She flung out a hand toward nowhere in particular.

He set down the duffel, shrugged out of his jacket and took off his hat, laying the jacket across the duffel and the hat on top of that. "Starr—"

She put up a hand. "Long flight, I bet. Thirsty? Sorry, I don't have any beer. But I have got fruit juice." She marched over to the kitchen nook and yanked open the refrigerator door. "Orange, grapefruit, pear...lots and lots of pear..."

"Starr..."

She shoved the door shut so hard he could hear the stuff inside clinking and rattling. "So. No juice, then. How about—?"

"Starr." He dared to take a step toward her. "Listen, I—"

"What?" She demanded, before he got a chance to finish. "Just...what?" He took another step. She narrowed her eyes at him and muttered. "Stop. Right there."

He stopped. "Starr, I only want—"

"You *know*," she accused through clenched teeth. "Admit it. Right now. You do, don't you? You *know*."

What could he say? The truth, he decided. They needed more truth between them. On her part—and on his, too. "Yeah. Yeah, I know."

"Tess broke my confidence." She folded her arms across her stomach.

Sweet God. He knew every soft, jasmine-scented inch of her body. And her body was...changing. There was a slight roundness to her belly. And her breasts were fuller...

Reality hit him all over again, swift and hard as a fist in the gut. She *was* going to have his baby.

He couldn't believe it.

He'd never been so happy.

He was absolutely terrified.

"She did," Starr insisted. "Tess broke her word to me."

"Er, not exactly..."

"What are you saying? She did or she didn't."

"Zach said—"

"Oh, wait. Let me guess. My dad. She told my dad and my dad—what? Showed up at Daniel's with a shotgun in his hands?"

He strove for reason. One of them had to. "Look, how I found out isn't what matters."

She had her lips pressed so hard together, they made a hard white line. "I can't...I don't..." She hung her shining head. He waited. He understood how she felt—well, maybe not exactly. But close enough. She looked up at last. And swallowed. "You know, I think I'd like to sit down."

He took another step toward her. By then, she was backed up against the sink. He dared to hold out a hand. "Come on," he whispered. "Please."

Slowly, she reached out and laid her hand in his.

They sat on the couch. She allowed him to put his arm around her and they sat there in silence for what seemed to him about a decade. He looked out the window at the skyscrapers across Central Park and waited for her to accept the fact that he was really here.

Eventually, she let him tell her that Zach had overheard Tess talking to her on the phone. "He told Tess that she'd better not call you, that you women had messed things up about enough and she'd damn well better give the men a chance to make this right."

Starr actually laughed at that. It was a pained kind of sound, but still. It *was* a laugh. Beau decided he'd take it as a good sign. "Poor Tess," she said. "Stuck in the middle, right where I put her. I hope she'll forgive me...."

"I'd imagine she's probably wondering if *you'll* forgive *her.*"

Starr leaned against him, then. He'd never felt anything so wonderful in his life—her soft sigh, the way her head rested in the crook of his shoulder.

He had her where she belonged—beside him—at last. This time, he was holding on. This time, she'd get neither cruel words nor cowardly denials from him.

She said, "Tess and I will work it out."

"Yeah. I know you will."

She lifted her head and looked at him then. "And what about us?"

He shrugged, though his heart was pounding so hard it felt like his chest was about to explode. "We'll go home," he said. "Get married. Be happy."

Her sweet lips trembled. "Because now you think you have to?"

"No. Because you love me—and I love you. Because I've always loved you. From that first second I saw you comin' toward me across your dad's front yard."

Her eyes were shining now. She sniffed, blinking

back the tears. "Suddenly loving me is enough, huh? It never was before."

He caught her shoulders, looked at her straight on. "Uh-uh. It was always enough. I was just too damn blind to see that. But even a blind man will get the picture eventually." She sniffed some more and swiped at her eyes. "You were right," he said, "about me blaming myself. Not so much for my dad and brothers. But for my mother..." His throat seized up. He had to cough into his hand before he could go on. "I guess I always felt like I should have done something to stop them from beating on her, that she needed help and I didn't give it, that I should have saved her somehow...."

She put her hand against his chest. "It wasn't your fault, Beau. You were a little kid." She said the words so softly.

He wrapped his hand around hers, brought it to his mouth, kissed the knuckles one by one. "I have something for you." He laid her hand on his chest once more—over the pocket of his shirt.

She frowned. "It feels like..."

He reached in, pulled out the thin gold chain. A heart-shaped locket twirled at the end of it. "It was hers—my mother's. Hold out your hand." She opened her palm and he dropped the locket into it.

She sniffled some more. "Oh, Beau..." She worked the tiny latch—and let out a small cry of dismay when she got it open. "But it's empty."

"Yeah. Once, a long time ago, there were pictures of my mom and dad in there."

"Where did they go?"

"Damned if I know. I guess you'll just have to supply the pictures yourself."

She was nodding now—with great enthusiasm. "Oh, I will. A picture of you and one of me—or maybe one of us together. That would leave the other side for the baby, when the baby comes...."

"Turn around." She shifted on the couch, showing him her back, lifting that curtain of midnight hair. He hooked the chain around her neck—and dared to press a quick kiss at her nape. "There."

She turned to him again, violet eyes gleaming. "It was in that envelope, wasn't it? The envelope of T.J.'s things..."

He gave her a slow smile then. "Got it all figured out, don't you?"

"Well. Was it?"

"Yeah," he confessed. "In his beat-up black wallet. He had twenty dollars in there and an expired driver's license—and that locket, tucked away in a hidden flap. I don't know how he got hold of it, but he had it. And now he's passed it on to me. That and my dad's old Timex. And a set of keys to a bunch of things that don't belong to T.J. anymore."

"You did it," she said. "You looked in that envelope. You dealt with what was in there."

"Well, yeah," he said, not all that impressed about it himself. "I did."

"Oh, Beau..." She sighed and swayed toward him, lifting her soft mouth to his.

With great effort, he held back from kissing her. "Is that a yes, then? Will you come home with me?"

"You're sure? It's what you really want?"

"More than you can ever know. Marry me. Be my

wife. We'll build ourselves a house next to Daniel's house and you can show me…what it can be. To have what matters—to be with you. To have a family.''

"Oh, Beau…''

"Say yes.''

And at last, she did. "Yes,'' she said. "I will marry you, Beau.''

He took the kiss she offered, then.

As he would take her love. And their baby.

Eagerly. With no holding back. No cruelty. And no denials.

For the rest of their lives.

From the Medicine Creek Clarion,
week of December 4 through December 10

Over The Back Fence
by
Mabel Ruby

It was a white wedding for Starr Bravo and Beau Tisdale just this past Saturday, December 1, at the Rising Sun Ranch, where the bride's family resides. The Reverend Applegate presided as the snow drifted down outside and the loving couple exchanged their sacred vows.

The wedding party, limited to close friends and family, repaired to the dining room after the vows to enjoy a hearty repast of Rising Sun beef and a wide array of side dishes, with a three-tiered wedding cake for dessert.

Bride and groom plan to build a new home at the Hart Ranch, where the groom is the foreman.

The bride, formerly of New York City, will be settling down to work full-time at our own *Medicine Creek Clarion*.

May we take this opportunity to wish you health, wealth, love and happiness, Beau and Starr, as you set forth on the great adventure known as married life!

★　★　★　★　★

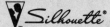

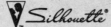

SPECIAL EDITION™

HER TEXAS RANGER

by

Stella Bagwell

(Silhouette Special Edition #1622)

Corinna Dawson had given up on the dream of
loving Seth Ketchum. But when the Texas Ranger
returned to his family's ranch to investigate
a murder, she knew a relationship with the rich
cowboy was no closer to reality than it had ever
been...until Seth vowed to change her mind.

**Whether ranchers or lawmen, these heartbreakers
can ride, shoot—and drive a woman crazy....**

Available July 2004 at your favorite retail outlet.

USA TODAY bestselling author

ERICA SPINDLER

Jane Killian has everything to live for. She's the toast of the Dallas art community, she and her husband, Ian, are completely in love—and overjoyed that Jane is pregnant.

Then her happiness shatters as her husband becomes the prime suspect in a murder investigation. Only Jane knows better. She knows that this is the work of the same man who stole her sense of security seventeen years ago, and now he's found her again… and he won't rest until he can *See Jane Die…*

SEE JANE DIE

"Creepy and compelling, *In Silence* is a real page-turner."
—New Orleans Times-Picayune

Available in June 2004 wherever books are sold.

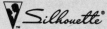

SPECIAL EDITION™

One family's search for justice begins in

ROMANCING THE ENEMY

(Silhouette Special Edition #1621)

by award-winning author
Laurie Paige

When beautiful Sara Carlton returns to her
hometown of San Francisco to avenge
her mother's death, she doesn't count on
falling in love with the handsome single father
next door—who just happens to be the son of
the enemy. Does she dare tell him the truth
about her return, or risk losing the love of
her life when he unravels the mystery?

The first book in the new continuity

The Parks Empire

**Dark secrets.
Old lies.
New loves.**

*Available July 2004
at your favorite retail outlet.*

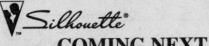

SPECIAL EDITION

#1621 ROMANCING THE ENEMY—Laurie Paige
The Parks Empire
Nursery school teacher Sara Carlton wanted to uncover the truth surrounding her father's mysterious death years ago, but when she met Cade Parks, the sexy son of the suspected murderer, she couldn't help but expose her heart. Could she shed the shadow of the past and give her love to the enemy?

#1622 HER TEXAS RANGER—Stella Bagwell
Men of the West
When summoned to solve a murder in his hometown, ruggedly handsome Ranger Seth Ketchum stumbled upon high school crush Corrina Dawson. She'd always secretly had her eye on him, too. Then all signs pointed to her father's guilt and suddenly she had to choose one man in her life over the other....

#1623 BABIES IN THE BARGAIN—Victoria Pade
Northbridge Nuptials
After Kira Wentworth's sister was killed, she insisted on taking care of the twin girls left behind. But when she and her sister's husband, Cutty Grant, felt an instant attraction, Kira found herself bargaining for more than just the babies!

#1624 PRODIGAL PRINCE CHARMING—Christine Flynn
The Kendricks of Camelot
Could fairy tales really come true? After wealthy playboy Cord Kendrick destroyed Madison O'Malley's catering truck, he knew he'd have to offer more than money if he wanted to charm his way toward a happy ending. But could he win the heart of his Cinderella without bringing scandal to her door?

#1625 A FOREVER FAMILY—Mary J. Forbes
Suddenly thrust into taking care of his orphaned niece and the family farm, Dr. Michael Rowan needed a helping hand. Luckily his only applicant was kind and loving Shanna McCoy. Close quarters bred a close connection, but only the unexpected could turn these three into a family.

#1626 THE OTHER BROTHER—Janis Reams Hudson
Men of the Cherokee Rose
While growing up, Melanie Pruitt had always been in love with Sloan Chisholm. But when she attended his wedding years later, it was his sexy younger brother Caleb who caught her attention. Both unleashed their passion, then quickly curbed it for the sake of friendship—until Melanie realized that she didn't need another friend, but something more....